PIRATE UTOPIA

DISCARD

— ALSO BY BRUCE STERLING —

Novels
Involution Ocean (1977)
The Artificial Kid (1980)
Schismatrix (1985)
Islands in the Net (1988)
The Difference Engine (with William Gibson) (1990)
Heavy Weather (1994)
Holy Fire (1996)
Distraction (1998)
Zeitgeist (2000)
The Zenith Angle (2004)
The Caryatids (2009)
Love Is Strange: A Paranormal Romance (2012)

Collections
Crystal Express (1989)
Globalhead (1992)
Schismatrix Plus (1996)
A Good Old-Fashioned Future (1999)
Visionary in Residence (2006)
Ascendancies: The Best of Bruce Sterling (2007)
Gothic High-Tech (2012)

Edited by
Mirrorshades: The Cyberpunk Anthology (1986)
Twelve Tomorrows (2014, 2015)

Nonfiction
The Hacker Crackdown: Law and Disorder on the Electronic Frontier (1992)
Tomorrow Now: Envisioning the Next Fifty Years (2002)
Shaping Things (2005)
The Epic Struggle of the Internet of Things (2014)

— ADDITIONAL PRAISE FOR PIRATE UTOPIA —

"★ Noted sci-fi maven and futurologist Sterling (*Love Is Strange*, 2012, etc.) takes a side turn in the slipstream in this offbeat, sometimes-puzzling work of dieselpunk-y alternative history. Resident in Turin, hometown of Calvino, for a dozen years, Sterling has long been experimenting with what the Italians call *fantascienza*, a mashup of history and speculation that's not quite science fiction but is kin to it. Take, for example, the fact that Harry Houdini once worked for the Secret Service, add to it the fact that H.P. Lovecraft once worked for Houdini, and *ecco*: why not posit Lovecraft as a particularly American kind of spook, "not that old-fashioned, cloak-and-dagger, European style of spy," who trundles out to Fiume to see what's what in the birthplace of Italian Futurism-turned-fascism? Lovecraft is just one of the historical figures who flits across Sterling's pages, which bear suitably futuristic artwork, quite wonderful, by British illustrator John Coulthart. Among the others are Woodrow Wilson and Adolf Hitler, to say nothing of Gabriele D'Annunzio and Benito Mussolini. "Seen from upstream, most previous times seem mad," notes graphic novelist Warren Ellis in a brief introduction, but the Futurist project seems particularly nutty from this distance; personified by Lorenzo Secondari, a veteran of World War I who leads the outlaw coalition called the Strike of the Hand Committee in the "pirate utopia" of the soi disant Republic of Carnaro, its first task is to build some torpedoes and then turn them into "radio-controlled, airborne Futurist torpedoes," not the easiest thing considering the technological limitations of the time. A leader of the "Desperates," who "came from anywhere where life was hard, but honor was still bright," Secondari and The Prophet—D'Annunzio, that is—recognize no such limitations and discard anything that doesn't push toward the future. So why not a flying pontoon boat with which to sail off to Chicago, and why not a partnership with Houdini to combat world communism? A kind of *Ragtime* for our time: provocative, exotic, and very entertaining." —*Kirkus*, starred review

"In *Pirate Utopia*, Bruce Sterling has brought off a minor miracle, an allegory on our present geopolitical *danza di morte* that doesn't feel remotely allegorical but instead stays true to its dieselpunk setting: a skewed Fiume crawling with Italian Futurists, Balkan anarcho-syndicalists, and demented Gernsbackian visionaries of all stripes and genders, their adventures documented through hilarious deadpan prose and John Coulthart's dazzling graphics." —James Morrow, author of *The Philosopher's Apprentice* and *The Madonna and the Starship*

— PRAISE FOR BRUCE STERLING —

He understands technology's present and future better than anyone in the field." —Cory Doctorow, author of *Little Brother*

"[Sterling's] highly caffeinated energy is hard to resist." —*Publishers Weekly*

"Breathtaking." —*New York Times Book Review*, on *The Difference Engine* (with William Gibson)

PIRATE
UTOPIA

BRUCE
STERLING

TACHYON

Introduction copyright © 2016 by Warren Ellis
Cast of Characters copyright © 2016 by Marty Halpern
"To the Fiume Station: Afterword"
copyright © by Christopher Brown
"Interview with Bruce Sterling"
copyright © 2016 by Rick Klaw
"Reconstructing the Future: Notes on Design"
copyright © 2016 by John Coulthart

Cover and interior art and design
copyright © 2016 by John Coulthart

Tachyon Publications
1459 18th Street #139
San Francisco, CA 94107
(415) 285-5615
TACHYON@TACHYONPUBLICATIONS.COM
WWW.TACHYONPUBLICATIONS.COM

Series Editor: Jacob Weisman
Editor: Marty Halpern
Project Editors: Rick Klaw and Jill Roberts

ISBN 13: 978-1-61696-236-4

Printed in the United States of America
by Worzalla

First Edition: 2016

9 8 7 6 5 4 3 2 1

★ CONTENTS ★

From where I

sit today, pirate coun-
try starts about ten miles east
of me. Foulness, Paglesham and the
Blackwater. To this day, pubs out there go
silent when a stranger walks in. You're standing on their dirt, after all. A life on the ocean
waves is one thing, but blood and soil are entirely
another.

Like the author of the marvelous little book you're
about to read, I work in the future. But, being British,
I also work in the past, because, being British, we don't
have a hell of a lot else to work with. We wrote our
stories big on the landscape here, in standing stones and

earthworks. Sea tales have nothing on the yarns we tell ourselves from dry land about the things to come.

Pirate utopias are a fiction, a social speculation spun out of stories of secret supply-base islands and anarchist colonies. The most famous, the fabled Libertatia of the 1600s, was probably invented pseudonymously by Daniel Defoe, downriver in London. And Defoe wasn't even his real last name. Fictions upon fictions upon fictions.

You may detect early on that more than one story is being told here.

Futurism, the business of the future, is the act of telling stories about what's next. Futurism, the movement, co-founded by F. T. Marinetti, was also, in its way, a story about blasting away the past and riding mad technology into fortune. Futurism was about speed, and machines, and, ultimately, blood and dirt. Marinetti's epiphany was crashing his car into a ditch to avoid some cyclists, emerging from the pit as a man of the Future, hell-bent on changing the course of history, celebrating war and scrubbing the world clean of freedom. He and his weird crew of poet-seers worked hard to export their mad dreams of velocity and gore abroad. But it had the smell of blood and dirt about it. The Russians wouldn't even let Marinetti talk when he came to put Moscow in motion— Cosmism was already murkily coursing around the country's veins, a strongly nationalist futurism of their own that put the homeland at the centre of a tomorrow devoted to bringing its sons and fathers back from death itself.

In this part of the world, futurism always seemed to come with nationalism. You needed a big old launchpad to operate the rockets of the new world from, and there are people today who will tell you it's a lot easier to land your spacecraft on dirt than boats.

The Cosmist dream has yet to come true. The Futurist dream did. It was World War One. Big story, launched off the back of a tangle of improbable coincidences. Which Marinetti fought, in some glorious ironic absurdity, on a bike—part of an Italian Army mountain cyclist unit. God knows how they did so well against the Austro-Hungarians. World War One succeeded in largely cleaning the Futurists from the world, their stories buried in trenches. Marinetti on his omen bicycle somehow survived, committed to Fascism, and by the time this story starts, he, having drafted the Italian Fascist Manifesto (because, like a good Futurist, he did love his manifestos), is about to withdraw from public life in a huff because his new friends didn't have enough forward speed. Reactionary elements were leaking into the enterprise, and, in his own future, Marinetti would give up to them in search of power in the new world.

In this same year, Marconi was firing the first radio entertainment broadcasts from Chelmsford, forty miles north of me, three years away from joining the Italian Fascist Party and ascending to government. It was a mad time. The sort of confluence that writers shake their heads dolefully at and intone, "If I'd tried to write that, people would never be able to suspend disbelief." But seen from upstream, most previous times seem mad.

★

This is the swirl of old gunsmoke, exterminating art and war dreams within which Bruce Sterling couches this story. It's always tempting to see mad times as a pivot point, around which ground lay the seeds of our own future. And this time is no different, set as it is on the streets of a pirate bay. I've read this book three or four times now, and perhaps the thing that pleases me most is that Bruce turns into the skid. It's a historical fiction that is fictionally true, a torpedo coursing through fact and fantasy and exploding as all possible stories and futures of the early Twentieth Century.

I do hope you enjoy this book as much as I did, relish its sly lessons on the nature of futurism, and cackle along with it as it takes flight into its dark cindery cloud of tomorrows gone by. Bruce Sterling always entertains, even when he's firing torpedoes at us.

Warren Ellis
Southend-On-Sea
27 February 2016

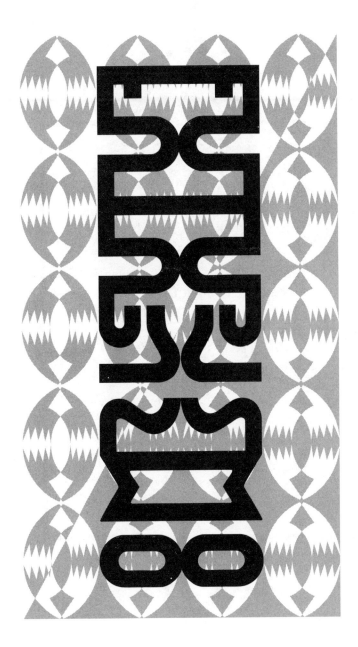

CAST OF CHARACTERS

THE REGENCY OF CARNARO

THE PROPHET [GABRIELE D'ANNUNZIO]: the military dictator of Fiume, its guiding light and great orator; renowned poet, Futurist Overman, and leader of the "Desperates."

THE CONSTITUTIONALIST [ALCESTE DE AMBRIS]: Carnaro's greatest political theorist.

THE ACE OF HEARTS [GUIDO KELLER]: The Prophet's right-hand man, and Secondari's patron in the Fiume secret police; a charismatic combat air ace and renowned expert in aerial reconnaissance.

LORENZO SECONDARI: The Pirate Engineer; former Army lieutenant and veteran of the Great War; gang-boss within the "Strike of the Hand Committee" (the fiercest pirate commandos of Fiume); later appointed Carnaro's Minister of Vengeance Weapons.

BLANKA PIFFER: The Pirate Engineer's business manager, interpreter, and purchasing agent; a Fiume native and Communist union leader; named "Corporate Syndicalist" and made dictator of her Torpedo Factory.

MARIA PIFFER: Blanka's seven-year-old daughter; a true native child of the Twentieth Century.

HANS PIFFER: Blanka's husband; abandoned Fiume after the Great War to join the Communist uprisings in Vienna; later ran off to Berlin where he joined a group of ex-soldiers and was arrested.

THE PIANIST [LUISA BACCARA]: The Prophet's mistress; a ferocious Venetian patriot and classical musician.

THE ART WITCH [LUISA CASATI]: a Milanese millionairesse, patroness of the arts, and occultist, who entertained The Prophet (another of his mistresses).

GIULIO ULIVI: a young visionary Italian radio engineer; discovered a new form of radiation which he named the "F-Ray."

BENITO MUSSOLINI: one of Carnaro's boldest allies; scandalous editor of the Milanese newspaper *Popolo d'Italia* (*People of Italy*); shot in the groin by his ex-wife.

VALENTINE DE SAINT-POINT: a Futurist dancing girl and companion of The Art Witch; participated in the attack on Mussolini with his ex-wife; author of the *Manifesto of Futurist Lust*.

ENRICO NOVELLI, AKA YAMBO: Genoese satirical cartoonist and journalist, best known for his boys' adventure books; succeeded Mussolini as editor of *Popolo d'Italia*.

GUGLIELMO MARCONI: an irascible one-eyed Italian radio genius and close personal friend of The Prophet; a Senator in the Italian government who took over as head of the technical caretaker government following the government's collapse.

THE UNITED STATES

WOODROW WILSON: President of the United States and tyrant of the League of Nations; gave Fiume away to Yugoslavia following the Great War, which resulted in the Fiume rebellion and the rise of the Regency of Carnaro; suffered a debilitating stroke while in office.

COLONEL [EDWARD M.] HOUSE: President Wilson's aide-de-camp, who now runs the government in Wilson's absence; a Texas gentleman and Army cavalier.

HARRY HOUDINI: The Man Without Fear; right-wing political activist and leader of the Secret Service spy delegation to the Regency of Carnaro; a magician of the black arts: "the greatest magician in the modern world."

HOWARD [H. P.] LOVECRAFT: Houdini's publicity agent and a member of the U.S. spy delegation.

ROBERT "BOB" ERVIN HOWARD: Houdini's teenage stage assistant and the third member of the U.S. spy delegation.

And Others

Adolf [Hitler]: a political extremist; during a beer-hall brawl he stepped in front of a bullet meant for Hans Piffer, thus giving his life to save another.

Joseph Goebbels: a political novelist; Hans Piffer's cellmate in Berlin who wrote a letter to Blanka Piffer on Hans's behalf.

Giuseppina "Pina" Menichelli: an Italian silent film diva.

Plus a cast of thousands of bewildered Adriatic townsfolk.

"Limit to courage? There is no limit to courage."
—*Gabriele D'Annunzio*

"I fear my enthusiasm flags when real work is demanded of me."
—*H. P. Lovecraft*

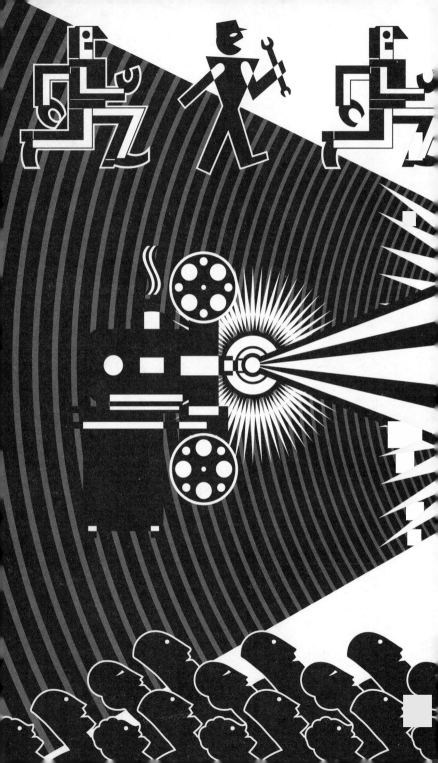

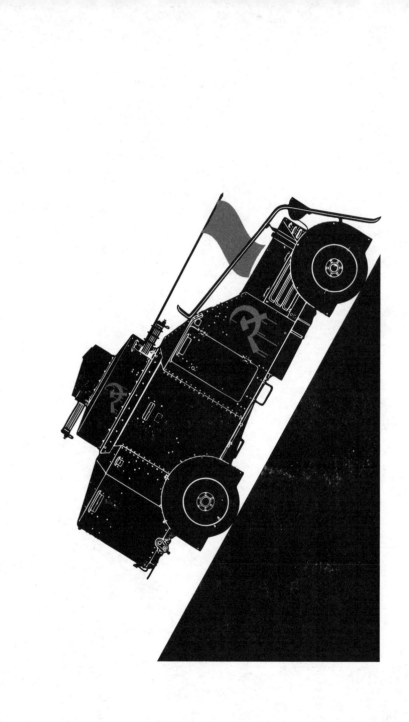

1: THE PIRATE CINEMA

I

OCCUPIED FIUME, JANUARY, 1920

TO CELEBRATE HIS
new, improved torpedo,
the engineer took his pirates to
the movies.

The spectacles in Futurist Fiume amazed the pirates. They'd never seen motion pictures.

The engineer's pirates were refugees and criminals. They felt rather shy about leaving their safe haven in the engineer's Torpedo Factory. To encourage themselves, they sang a Croatian sea ditty and whistled loudly at the passing girls.

Using his cane, the engineer wobbled along in the wake of his nine pirate crewmen. His female companion helped him over a tangled mess of harbor rope. Frau Blanka Piffer was a native of Fiume. She served as the engineer's business manager, interpreter, and purchasing agent.

The pirates left the dockside, with its dense mass of cranes, quays, and railway tracks. Downtown Fiume had a stone broadway with tall, peculiar gas-lamps. The church and the clock tower were the tallest buildings in the town.

The Croatian pirates were vividly conspicuous. All nine of them wore stolen women's fur overcoats, cinched by thick leather army belts festooned with daggers, pistols, and hand grenades.

As the pirates swaggered by, the dames of Fiume fled inside the dress-shops. The gentlemen dropped their news-papers and abandoned their sidewalk cafés. Children hid themselves behind the horse-carts and fruit-stands. Even stray dogs ran off.

Frau Piffer tugged the engineer's black sleeve. "Lorenzo: did you have to bring all these crooks to the movies with us? I thought we were going alone."

"I told you to bring the daughter along," said the engi-neer, reading her lips.

"I won't take my innocent child to see that man-eater!" said Frau Piffer. "Your Turinese femme fatale!"

"Pina Menichelli is from Naples," the engineer correct-ed. "You mustn't fuss about cinema, my dear. The Prophet himself adores the movies. He wrote the script of *Cabiria,* the greatest motion picture ever filmed! Made in Turin, of course."

Frau Piffer pursed her small, red lips, but she obeyed him.

Blanka Piffer was a Communist union leader. When the Great War had ended, her Torpedo Factory had been shuttered. Frau Piffer had lost both her livelihood and her husband, for Herr Piffer was an Austrian Communist agitator. Herr Piffer had abandoned Fiume and run off to join the violent uprisings in Red Vienna.

Frau Piffer's Torpedo Factory in Fiume had become a gloomy Red Cross depot, where Frau Piffer doled out soup to her despairing factory girls.

Then the engineer had arrived in Fiume from Italy, intent on saving the day. The engineer was Lieutenant Lorenzo Secondari, a veteran of the Royal Artillery, Third Army.

Secondari had spent four years on the front lines of Isonzo, maintaining Italy's war machinery. Constantly improvising under harsh battlefield conditions, making do with scrap, rivets, and steel wire, Secondari had deftly repaired Italian howitzers, trench mortars, FIAT trucks, pneumatic drills, even military telephones and radios.

Being from Turin, Lieutenant Secondari fully understood the needs of heavy industry. Once he'd met Frau Piffer inside her Torpedo Factory——(they had met because he was hungry, and he needed the Red Cross soup)——he'd been appalled to see such a splendid assembly line standing idle.

At his shouted insistence——Secondari was deaf from wartime cannon fire, so he tended to shout whenever he spoke——Frau Piffer's Communist factory workers had declared a strike. They seized their empty Torpedo Factory and placed it under worker occupation.

Secondari re-commenced local arms production with the simplest, most humble weapons he could create. These

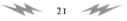

guns were crude single-shot derringers, punched from sheet-metal. The guns used ten-penny nails as firing pins, and they tended to burst.

He paid the striking workers with the flimsy handguns. The factory girls then swapped and bartered the guns with all the other women in Fiume.

The Torpedo Factory busily made hundreds of these cheap, nameless guns until the factory's owner had shown up, and urged the workers to desist. Whining in his bourgeois, conformist fashion, this rich man had complained that the Great War was all over. He'd said that it was morally wrong to make more weapons in peacetime.

Secondari had seized the capitalist, beaten him up, shaved his head, and dosed him with castor oil. The wretch had fled Fiume for Switzerland, never to return.

Secondari's Futurist fervor profoundly inspired the factory girls. Liberated by this swift change in their circumstances, they became eager factory pirates.

These female assembly workers found ways to re-purpose their factory tools, to illicitly copy the objects of their own desires. The girls happily banged out steel pots, pans, tableware, and kitchen stoves. They also redoubled their production of grenades and sea-mines.

The factory's weapons found ready buyers, as the Occupation persisted and the rebel soldiers dug in. American men with Irish accents arrived in civilian sailboats. They took the sea-mines to torment Great Britain, and they paid with American dollars.

Some Turks arrived, too: clean-shaven fanatics from the

insurgent army of Mustafa Kemal. These "Young Turks" were Western-educated Moslem rebels. They bought grenades and car-bombs, and they paid with black opium.

With this money in her hands, Frau Piffer transformed her dull, brick war-factory into a vibrant stronghold of Futurist feminism. Frau Piffer's communal assembly line featured cake socials, tea breaks, and a generous child-care policy. Her factory's public address system played American jazz records.

The leaders of Occupied Fiume were poets and political radicals, but they had to notice so much innovation and initiative. Lieutenant Secondari and Frau Piffer were both well-rewarded. Secondari was made a gang-boss within the "Strike of the Hand Committee," the fiercest pirate commandos of Fiume. Frau Piffer was transformed into a "Corporate Syndicalist," and made the dictator of her factory.

For their night together, out on the town, Frau Piffer wore her shining new Syndicalist ensemble, granted to her by the grateful Fiume regime. Frau Piffer's Futurist paramilitary outfit had dazzling zigzag lines in shades of Italian orange, white, and green, plus a shining silk sash heavy with bronze medallions.

Frau Piffer was portly, married, and eleven years older than Secondari. Frau Piffer was an ugly, older woman from a newer, better world.

"It might be best if Maria avoids *Cabiria*," Secondari mused. "I just remembered a scene in that movie where a little girl is flung into the flaming belly of a brazen beast-god."

"We should see *Cabiria* together some night soon," Frau Piffer urged. "You work much too hard, Lorenzo. Every night you're out on those raiding boats, stealing diesel fuel. You should see more of the local people. Try to make some real friends."

"Oh, *Cabiria* is just a peacetime movie," said Secondari. "I don't care a damn about the ancient past."

The pirates arrived at the movie house. This Fiume cinema was a small musical-comedy theater. It sat within a modest piazza, crowded with glum examples of bad provincial Austro-Hungarian architecture.

The ticket-seller was a teenage girl. She had insolent bobbed hair, narrow plucked brows, and scarlet lipstick. She sat within a glass booth, reading a cheap German romance novel. Muffled jazz music blasted from her radio set.

Since Secondari was half-deaf, he hated conversing with the locals of Fiume. In fact, Secondari hated leaving his Torpedo Factory for any reason at all, except for enthusiastic pirate raids. Using low-slung, rapid Italian assault boats, his "Strike of the Hand Committee" raided the whole Adriatic. Half spies and half black-marketeers, operating mostly on moonless nights, the utopian pirates of Fiume stole supplies from half-abandoned Great War military depots. Secondari knew exactly what to steal, so he went along on every pirate raid. He generally manned a cannon.

Secondari brusquely rapped at the glass ticket-booth with the brass head of his gentleman's cane. "Miss, I built that radio with my own hands! So turn it off and pay attention to me."

The startled girl dropped her romance book. She struggled with the dials of her wooden radio box. The jazz music grew much louder, and the ticket-girl shouted in dismay.

"My gallant troops are here to see your movie!" Secondari bellowed at her. "Let us all in at once!"

The ticket-seller pointed angrily at the clock-tower, then at the nine Croat pirates, who were puffing smuggled Turkish cigarettes and knocking mud from their jackboots.

Secondari threw open his trenchcoat, revealing a black shirt, black jodhpur trousers, a bandolier of grenades, two holstered Glisenti semi-automatics, and a trench dagger the size of his forearm.

He plucked a newspaper clipping from his wallet, which was stuffed with five kinds of currency. "Now, you see here, miss! Your own advertisement states—no, look at this clipping, it's from yesterday's issue of *The Fiume Head of Iron*—it distinctly states that Miss Menichelli's feature begins at five pm!"

"Let me talk to her," said Frau Piffer.

Secondari stepped aside.

"Ciao, Tanja!" Frau Piffer chirped. "Is that Barney Bigard and his Jazzopators? They're great, aren't they? Turn that down a little! Use that big brown knob."

The ticket-seller successfully reduced the radio jazz racket. She made some muffled remark about Frau Piffer's new uniform.

"I'm a Corporate Syndicalist nowadays," Frau Piffer announced, preening at her lapels.

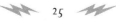

"So, what's that?" silently mouthed the ticket-girl, from behind her glass.

"Well, I don't know that yet! You'll have to ask the Constitutionalist about that! He's a genius!"

The ticket-girl made some flippant remark to the effect that all the leaders of Occupied Fiume were geniuses, but all the geniuses had to pay to watch her movies, anyway.

"Now Tanja, your father is a good Communist, isn't he? So why don't you let us inside there, without some exchange of cash? We're from the Torpedo Factory! I could see to it that you and your girlfriends get some very nice little pistols."

Tanja the ticket-girl twirled one kiss-curl over her lacquered fingernail. She then boasted about the Italian soldiers who were already inside her theater, happily watching her movies.

The Occupation troops of Fiume were the Arditi, the Alpini, and the legendary Royal Grenadiers of Sardinia. These fierce Italian elite troops feared no man and adored all women.

Frau Piffer stiffened. "You'd better watch that tongue of yours, young lady! Lieutenant Secondari is my business associate! Our relationship is entirely chaste and revolutionary."

Vividly waving her hands behind the glass, Tanja scoffed.

Frau Piffer then switched to speaking German. Being a Fiume girl, Tanja also spoke excellent German.

Since Fiume was an Italo-Balkan port city, the people of Fiume spoke an entire Babel of tongues. Unfortunately, the Great War had smashed Secondari's right ear. Even when the Fiumans spoke good Italian, Secondari was hard-put to hear them. He entirely failed to understand their Serbo-Croatian speech. Their Hungarian was a profound mystery to him.

The rich people of Fiume spoke some French, but Secondari hated the arrogant rich, and didn't much like the French, either. The English language was well known in Fiume's banking and shipping circles. Secondari could speak and write English rather well. However, the Great War had deafened him. Civilian life would always be a conspiracy to him.

The two Fiume women rattled along, parrying and bargaining, as if selling fish. The city life of Fiume was kinked like tarry harbor rope with Gordian knots of this kind. Secondari's thoughts drifted toward Futurism, as his thoughts generally did.

His next logical step was entirely clear to him. He had to manufacture naval torpedoes—that should be easy, in a Torpedo Factory—and then some radio-controlled, airborne Futurist torpedoes.

In Turin, Italy's national plans for flying torpedoes were gathering dust in the blueprint drawers of the War Ministry. Many brilliant Italian military innovations had been sadly doomed by the Armistice.

The new civilian government in Rome was weak, impoverished, and gutless. The civilians had mutilated Italy's great victory during the Great War. They were trying to put the Great War behind them, instead of ahead of them, where it properly belonged.

The secret agents of the Fiume "Strike of the Hand Committee" would steal those flying torpedo plans from inside Italy. Then Secondari would illicitly copy these un-built war-machines within his pirate factory.

The Anarcho-Syndicalist city-state would then own and brandish flying Futurist torpedoes. Even a civilian fool could see that this feat would change the destiny of the world.

Lorenzo Secondari was not an inventor. He lacked the creative skills for that. Instead, he was what he most want-ed to be: a free pirate. Given the stolen plans, he had no doubt that he could successfully build flying radio torpe-does. Anyone who doubted his capacities deserved a hard lesson.

Frau Piffer glanced up from her negotiations. "Do you have any ready-money, Lorenzo?"

"Aha! Yes, indeed I do! Tell this tawdry creature that I have a good stock of American dollars."

"Dollars are only good for buying dynamite," Frau Piffer mourned. "Do you have any postage stamps?"

Secondari scowled. The Revolution had been selling its exotic postage stamps to foreigners, ever since the anar-chist liberation of September 1919. Along with drugs, jazz music, and easy divorce, the postage stamp racket was a way of scraping by. The Fiumans often used their postage stamps as their makeshift internal currency.

"Postage stamps always stick inside my wallet," Secondari complained. He selected a legitimate British five-pound note from among a sheaf of fake ones. The Fiume

"Strike of the Hand Committee" was wonderfully adept at forgery. However, British currency notes were hard work.

"Five pounds is much too much money!" Frau Piffer said. "She would have to give you change in dinars."

"Dinars! Outrageous!" Secondari yelled. "The 'Kingdom of Yugoslavia' cannot exist! I should arrest her for offering me Yugoslav money."

The impatient Croat pirates were shuffling at the delay. Some of Fiume's ubiquitous street urchins had shown up. They were begging the pirates for cigarettes.

One of the Croat pirates tossed his fine fur coat into the gutter. He tore his blue-striped nautical shirt from his tattooed back. He handed this to a young boy.

Secondari was not to be outdone by this splendid revolutionary gesture. He picked up the pirate's fur coat, dusted it off, cordially handed it back, then gave the Croat his favorite Swiss Army knife, direct from his own pocket.

He then confronted Frau Piffer. "Get this mess over with," he ordered.

Frau Piffer shouted at length at the ticket-seller, who was rebellious, but unable to resist a uniformed adult. "All right," Frau Piffer said at last. "I've fixed it. We'll give her some jazz records, later."

"Good work."

"We'll have to sit upstairs in the balcony. No gunfire. Also no brandy, no pipes, and no cigars."

Frau Piffer distributed the movie tickets to the pirates, then bought them nine boxes of popcorn. The happy marauders settled upstairs into the cheap seats, jostling their

pistol belts and scratching at flea-bites. They immediately began smoking.

"Turin has movie palaces five times the size of this place," Secondari griped. "I should steal this theater! I could run pirated movies in here."

"Lorenzo, have you been snorting cocaine again?"

"No, I haven't," Secondari lied. The Ace of Hearts, his patron in the Fiume secret police, had given him a steady supply of the useful Peruvian herb. All the flying aces made much use of cocaine. Cocaine sharpened the senses for combat.

Newsreels commenced on the silver movie screen. These newsreels were American in origin because American newsreels were everywhere, and therefore easy to steal.

The first newsreel concerned American big-game hunters in Africa. The second reel featured "Tarzan." Tarzan was the American version of a Nietzschean Overman. Tarzan was a superhuman anarchist, but since he lived in a jungle, he did not have to smash the State.

The feature began, and the theater's hired pianist played along. Secondari scarcely heard the tinkling piano, but he did not mind. Since it was silent, the cinema was the one form of modern art in which a deaf man could fully participate.

The Turinese film featured the famous diva, Pina Menichelli, as a Russian countess, exiled and living in Italy. La Menichelli was a gorgeous creature of aristocratic privilege, from a fabulous Czarist world of sables and diamonds.

Of course her noble Russian life had been shattered by the Twentieth Century. The Russian Countess had wandered to Turin, bearing the livid infection of her doom, and the Italian noblemen within her high social circle... They were all degenerate dabblers and dilettantes. Feeble, nerveless, archaic dolts with slicked-back hair, celluloid collars, and boiled shirt-fronts. Not one of these despicable toffs and weaklings had any Futurism to offer to this beautiful woman.

As the tragic film progressed, the Countess devoured these wretches like a female Moloch. Then she turned her fatal rage upon herself. Secondari was stirred to his core.

Until he'd left Torino for the revolution in Fiume, he had never realized that his own Kingdom of Italy was so entirely like Czarist Russia. But the Fiume Revolution had raised his political awareness. Italy, just like Russia, had a weakling King, a rotten Parliament, and a starved population. One rush and a push by hard and determined men, and Rome would topple into its own streets.

As for La Menichelli, her director and her screenwriter could not save the actress from her bitter fate. Wafting across her silent screen, Pina Menichelli was a silver ghost: a lovely creature from some better world that had been denied existence.

The tragedy was hard to bear, but it was followed by a short, comic two-reeler: *An Interplanetary Romance*. This low-budget diversion concerned an Italian gent in love with a pretty girl from Mars.

The sprightly comedy was directed by "Yambo," a Genoese journalist best known for his boys' adventure books. Yambo's movie was ingenious, but it had been filmed on the cheapest kind of celluloid. The movie jammed on its metal reel, bubbling and smoking. The silver screen went stark white.

The usher had to apologize to the indignant movie crowd—restive Italian soldiers, mostly, along with their screeching local girlfriends. To calm them, the usher hastily offered up a makeshift song and dance, along with the theater's pianist.

The dancing usher was quickly hooted off the stage. The resourceful management somehow located a radically different act: a blind poet with a fiddle. This bearded Balkan derelict wailed away with his bow on the single taut wire of his instrument.

His eerie peasant racket was unbearable, even for a deaf man. The Italian troops were leaving the theater in disgust. Secondari also rose from his plush seat.

"Sit down now, he can sing," Frau Piffer protested. "It's a beautiful language, once you know it."

"I prefer the Slavs silent," Secondari said. He rose and shuffled past his line of nine Croat pirates, who were staring at the blind singer and wiping their tearful eyes.

Frau Piffer obediently followed him. They collected her Futurist hat in the lobby.

"You sure did stare at that pretty actress," she told him.

"La Menichelli? She's a goddess! She's a diva, a Nietzschean superhuman! Imagine dying in the embrace of a gorgeous creature like that!"

"I never heard you talk that way before."

"You never took me to a movie before."

"Well, I suppose that you like girls well enough, then. If they are your Turinese movie-star girls."

"I have no time for women in my life, you know all that." Secondari shrugged. "Forget it. I'm hungry now. I have some money. Thank God the blockade is over. Let's go eat something nice, in a nice place."

"What good ideas you have sometimes, Lorenzo! I know such a nice place for the two of us! My cousin cooks there. We'll have some squid first, a soup, a pasta, then we can share some baked bronzin.... My cousin will be so nice to us. He never makes any scandals...." Frau Piffer cheerily pushed open the door to the piazza. She instantly went pale with terror.

Secondari glanced outside, over Frau Piffer's gaudy, striped, Syndicalist shoulder. During the movie show, some Communists had gathered outside, in a typical Communist street demonstration.

These local malcontents, to judge by their pickets and banners, were the staffers from Fiume's oil refinery. Their oil refinery was sitting derelict, since the League of Nations had denied Fiume any shipments of crude oil.

"You're a Communist yourself, my dear," he said to Frau Piffer. "So why are you afraid of these fools?"

"Because these are Bolsheviki, they're Leninists! My cell is from Red Vienna." Frau Piffer put one plump hand to her waxed red lips. "And what if they see me now, in my Futurist outfit? Oh my God! Quick, give me your trench-coat! There must be some back way out of here."

Secondari barked with laughter. In Turin, the Communist demonstrations were huge, raging seas of angry industrial workers. The Fiume demonstration outside was maybe thirty local people. They were carefully parking their bicycles, and readying some silly drums and whistles.

The oil workers were all draft dodgers. They all had industrial deferments. They'd never heard one shot fired in anger in the Great War. They were scarcely men at all.

"Go and fetch my pirates from upstairs," he told Frau Piffer. "We'll scatter those small-town Commies like mice."

"Oh no, please, don't shoot them! These are my own friends and neighbors! Oh look, there's Tanja's dad—that nice Signor Adelardi! I didn't know he'd become a Bolshevik now! That's terrible!"

Secondari sighed. He shrugged out of his trenchcoat, and gallantly fitted it over the gaudy Syndicalist uniform of Frau Piffer. His trenchcoat's shoulders hung halfway to Frau Piffer's elbows. The coat's hem dragged along the theater floor.

"Do you feel any better now?" he said. Frau Piffer nodded mutely. Frau Piffer ruled her female factory workers with a rod of iron, but outside her own gates, she was as meek as a nun.

A cluster of Italian soldiers left the movie house. Secondari joined them. He wandered freely through the crowd of Communist protesters.

Secondari was a Fiume Revolutionary pirate. Therefore, he always wore black. He wore black jackboots, a thick black shirt, black puttees, and black jodhpur pantaloons.

For special revolutionary occasions, Secondari had a black kepi hat, and a black cummerbund to wrap around his waist. Secondari had worn this all-black ensemble ever since joining the "Desperates." He didn't own any other form of clothing.

Secondari also carried two Glisenti nine-millimeter automatic pistols, a razor-sharp Arditi dagger, and three live trench grenades. No one in the busy crowd took any notice of him. They didn't recognize him personally, or care about his weapons.

Secondari lifted his cane. This handsome Turinese gentleman's cane had once belonged to his late grandfather. He used this creation of teak, iron, and brass to beckon sarcastically at Frau Piffer.

She crouched behind the theater door in her pathetic fear. Frau Piffer had her virtues, but boldness was not among them.

But the Communists had grown bolder. They banged drums and shrieked with whistles, but since Secondari was deaf, he was spared most of the noise.

The Marxists were harmless fools. Just because a few Jews and Freemasons had seized Moscow, they imagined that Communism would rule the whole world some day.

The Communists were distributing Marxist propaganda. Secondari accepted a broadsheet, from a weedy Fiume civilian with a red star pasted onto his jaunty straw boater hat.

Secondari glanced over the cheap, grimy paper. It was their usual Commie rubbish about justice, class struggle, and the labor theory of value. The Communists had been saying the same things since the remote 1840s. How could that quaint rubbish possibly be Futurism?

Two of the burlier Communists passed him, carrying a banner-sign strung from two tall wooden poles. "DEATH TO THE SOUTH SLAV COMMITTEE OF AGRAM." Who was that? Who cared? What difference could it make to the world?

Police arrived to oversee the growing tumult. General Vadala's Italian police were under military command.

Secondari heartily despised the Occupation police. He hated all police everywhere, because he was a pirate.

His immediate superior in piracy was the Ace of Hearts. The Ace of Hearts was the head of the revolutionary secret police. The secret police in Fiume were secrets even to the Italian military police.

Annoyed by the capering Communists, Secondari wobbled back into the theater. The night air had grown colder, and his bad ear was aching sharply. His interior sense of balance was disturbed by his war wound. He leaned with care on his grandfather's cane.

He found Frau Piffer in an anxious conclave with the teenaged ticket-seller.

"Aren't you satisfied yet?" he interrupted. "Let's go eat dinner."

"The Communists came here to kill all the Croats," said Frau Piffer. "Because the Croats are Yugoslavs."

The ticket-seller pursed her sticky red lips—she had the same tint as Frau Piffer's own lipstick, and probably the same black-market supplier. Speaking in German, she suddenly emitted a startling stream of hatred. Her crazy rant had something to do with Croats, and Yugoslavia, and gunfire in the streets, and war atrocities.

"You two girls lack proper political awareness," said Secondari, in Italian. "My pirates aren't Yugoslav royalists, they're Croatian nationalists! They hate Yugoslavia much more than you two little ladies do."

"Didn't I tell you to hide those ugly brutes in the factory?" cried Frau Piffer, shivering in terror. "Croats can't march around Fiume like they own this town!"

"But Blanka, you yourself are a Croat!" said Secondari, losing his tact. "'Blanka' is a Croatian name! And you, there, you little movie girl—'Tanja,' what kind of name is that? You're not Italian either!"

Shamefaced, the ticket-seller muttered something inaudible.

"But we're all Italians now!" Frau Piffer insisted. "The mob will kill those dirty foreigners like dogs."

The ticket-seller lifted her chin, spoke Italian, and solemnly promised that everyone would be murdered as soon as her next feature let out.

Secondari glanced at the miserable street demonstration. His temper was fraying. Why was Fiume so like this, so full of minute, antlike struggle?

There was no real fight to be found around here, in that cobbled plaza with its cheap billiard halls and bad restaurants.

Secondari knew what a genuine war looked like. He'd been in the world's greatest war for four years. Real war meant bayoneting Austrian Jaeger troops in trenches dynamited from frozen Alpine granite. That was real warfare. Militant Communist oil workers were soft, portly, middle-aged idiots with retirement plans.

An armored car rolled upon the scene. "Hey, wait!" Secondari said. "That's not fair."

This armored car had been stolen from the regular Italian army. Almost every piece of military equipment in Revolutionary Fiume had been stolen from Italy.

It had not occurred to Secondari that the political factions inside Fiume would steal Italian weapons from their own pirate regime. But the Communists had done exactly that. The local Communists had pirated an Italian armored car. It was five meters long and as tall as a two-story building.

Secondari hadn't given the Communists any permission to behave as pirates. He found their crime intensely annoying. The stolen armored car—a standard Lancia-Ansaldo IZM, of the 1918 vintage—was ridiculously defaced. A red hammer and sickle had been sloppily daubed onto its turret. A red battle-flag was lashed to the muzzle of the turret's heavy machine-gun.

Secondari left the cinema, wobbling quickly on his cane. He shouldered his way through the drum-beating, whistling crowd of Communists, until he reached the elongated metal bulk of the armored car. He hauled himself aboard it.

A young civilian oil worker was perched high in the turret. He was leaning down to flirt with a pretty girl in the crowd.

Secondari poked the Marxist with the iron ferrule of his cane. "Get out," he ordered.

"What?" the Communist said.

"Get out of this Lancia vehicle, you can't have it."

The young Communist spoke to the crew deep inside the armored car. He bent down and grabbed something as they handed it up to him. It was a pistol.

The Communist tried to chamber a round. Secondari plucked a grenade from his own belt. He pulled the pin and dropped the grenade into the car.

The Communists scrambled from the vehicle, screaming. Secondari waited for the grenade to burst. He used his left hand to shield his one good ear.

The grenade failed to detonate. It was a factory second. The Torpedo Factory had built a dud.

Disappointed by this, Secondari climbed into the Lanzia. He slammed and latched the turret door. He found the dud grenade, which had rolled under the skeletal metal seat. The grenade looked all right, but some factory girl had failed to arm it correctly. Secondari slipped the loose pin back into the bomb, and attached it to his bandolier.

Then he gunned the Lancia's huge engine. He grabbed the crowbar-sized stick-shift, and jammed the armored car into first gear.

He then rolled briskly through the piazza, scattering the panicking Communists. He chased down the most stubborn and reluctant ones, crushing their banners and drums beneath the Lanzia's colossal tires. The Marxists recognized the trend, despite their belief in historical materialism. They ran away.

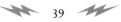

Secondari then parked the armored car beside the movie theater. A bemused crowd of Alpini were observing the scene. The Alpini were not scared of an armored car, because the Alpini weren't scared of anything. However, they didn't know what to make of the situation.

Secondari popped the turret open and hauled himself half-out, head and shoulders.

"Do any of you beloved combat comrade sons of bitches want to give me any trouble tonight?" he shouted.

Slowly, the Alpini applauded him. Some doffed their feathered Alpine hats in respect. Others whistled, and the biggest one, who was staggering drunk, even yodelled.

"Send out those flea-bitten Croat bastards of mine! And if any Commie son-of-a-whore wants to quarrel with the deaf man here"—Secondari pounded his own chest with his fist—"you can tell those faggots to come storm my factory gates! You understand that?"

The Alpini understood this quite well. They were touched to hear such salty battlefield language again. They had heard men speak like that every day during the Great War, but civilians never spoke realistically.

After a brief delay and confusion, the nine Croatian pirates sheepishly emerged from the movie house. They climbed onto the steep, armored hull of Secondari's armored car.

Secondari then drove his pirates down the silent streets of Fiume. Nobody offered any trouble to him. The armored car was entirely his own.

He parked the stolen car next to the other trophies he had piled in the factory's assembly yard. Armored flame-throwers.

Pneumatic drills for mountain warfare. Great spidery heaps of disused radio antennas. So many awesome and efficient things that a stricken world had bent every possible effort to build, and then forgotten.

2: THE ACE OF HEARTS

II
THE GREAT WAR,
1914–1918

ONLY HEROIC SUPER-
MEN would defy the whole
world from a modest Adriatic
town called "Fiume."

The name "Fiume" simply meant
"River," or "Rijeka," in Croatian. The Italian
folk of "River" lived mostly on the western
bank of their river, while the Balkan Croatians of
"Rijeka" clung mostly to their river's eastern bank.

The ancient river of Fiume/Rijeka flowed from
tall, obscure, and barren mountains where millions of
Italian and Austrian soldiers had recently been killed.
The river of River always had pure, clean water. The river of River never ran dry.

Futurism had brought Lorenzo Secondari to this river,
because he was a heroic superman. Fiume was the spiritual capital of the greatest event of the Twentieth Century.

He, Lorenzo Secondari, was there among the future's Men of Destiny.

Secondari had long treasured this superhuman idea about himself. Since he was Turinese, he had read Friedrich Nietzsche during his high school days. Nietzsche had written his best works inside the city of Turin. Nietzsche was therefore the favorite philosopher of restless Turinese teenagers.

After reading Nietzsche, on the subject of the Overman, and the Overman's high-minded scorn for the slave mentality delimited by "good" and "evil," Secondari had recognized that the everyday world was quite unworthy of him, too. He hadn't said much about this personal conviction, however. He was a teenage boy from Turin, so race-cars and airplanes interested him much more than philosophical aspirations did.

The Great War had changed everything about that, however. In the Great War, the superhuman Lorenzo Secondari had been killed.

On the fateful afternoon of November 22, 1917, an Austrian mortar round had struck and killed Secondari during an artillery duel on the icy heights of the Adamello front.

The Austrian mortar's concussion had blown the life right out of the body of Lorenzo Secondari. Secondari was entirely clear about this experience. He remembered every vivid detail.

Lorenzo Secondari was unsurprised to find himself dead in battle. He had rather expected to die as a soldier, for Lorenzo Secondari had successfully killed a huge number of enemy Austrians. Secondari had, in fact, deliberately joined the Italian artillery corps in order to efficiently exterminate the maximum number of Austrians.

Being Piedmontese, Secondari understood the historical role of Piedmont in destroying Austro-Hungarian despotism. Members of his family had been fighting the Austrians for centuries. His ancestors had consecrated their lives to an Austrian defeat.

In this vast historical struggle, Lieutenant Lorenzo Secondari had fallen. He was one among five million similarly dead Italian soldiers. He had paid the last, full price of his patriotic devotion.

So he was dead in the Alps, with his soul floating outside his shattered mortal body.

However, the army medic within Secondari's military unit was from Turin, just like himself. This gifted young doctor was a student of Turin's greatest medical scientist: Cesare Lombroso.

Using Lombroso's psychically advanced séance techniques— (for the first time ever employed on a battlefield)— this Turinese medic had contacted Secondari's wandering soul. The doctor had restored the soul to Secondari's still-warm corpse.

This gifted Turinese doctor had also been killed by the Austrian artillery, a mere six days later. So the battlefield medic had never found the time or opportunity to inform anyone of his feat. During the Great War, many acts of similar heroism had gone unrecorded by authority.

However, Secondari was entirely clear and lucid about the matter. He remembered his death in combat. He

remembered his resuscitation by the doctor. He remembered that the Italian Army, using an iron spiderweb of "teleferica" ski-lifts, had reeled him downhill from the frozen mountain height.

Secondari had silently plummeted, swaying and reeling, without one whisper of noise, down, down, down, to the world beyond his battlefield. Then he lay on his canvas stretcher and silently bled, until a Red Cross ambulance, silent, came.

That silent journey, he also remembered with great clarity. The silent ambulance was full of Italian wounded and dying, and driven by an American volunteer. They'd spoken some English together, he and the American driver, as the medic handled Secondari's blood-soaked stretcher. The American's mustached lips had moved, but without a sound.

Many days later, back in Turin, in a drab hotel transformed into a military hospital, Secondari lay alone in his cot. He was alive in a great and lasting silence. He had broken ribs, a shattered collarbone, and thirty-eight large and small shrapnel wounds. His right ear no longer existed. It had been torn from his head.

Secondari was heavily sedated, yet in full, intimate contact with vast, swirling panoplies of mystical reality. Day by day, tormented by his many wounds, Secondari revived. He writhed in fevered anguish during Caporetto, the worst Italian defeat of the Great War. He regained his feet during Vittorio Veneto, when the Italian Army conclusively destroyed Italy's thousand-year-old imperial enemy. The Empire of Austria-Hungary was swept from the map of Europe. It was no more.

The Great War ended. Austria-Hungary's dead remains were a rabble of new republics. The fallen Empire of Germany was also a new republic. The victorious Kingdom of Italy remained a Kingdom.

For Lieutenant Lorenzo Secondari, the peacetime world of the victorious Kingdom of Italy was a ghostly place. It was almost silent. Lieutenant Secondari, war veteran, could still read and write. He could scarcely hear a word.

His balance was gone because his inner ear was wrecked, but when he used his dead grandfather's cane, he could walk, well enough.

He returned to engineering school for a while, where he could not hear the lectures properly. He frequented the school's library, where he sat alone, reading the latest English-language magazines, about popular science and popular mechanics. These American magazines had grown quite strange, since the Great War had ended. The Americans were full of plans to build personal radios, and plans to build personal airplanes. Nothing built for a king or a nation, everything built for one man.

The harried military doctors wrote an official letter to Secondari. They predicted that his left ear would get better. It did, somewhat: because there was dull roaring, then ringing, and then, one day, he heard coherent sound. His right ear scarcely existed, but sometimes he heard noise with it, mostly while dreaming.

The Italian Army demobilized Secondari. He found himself among a new Italian army, the shabby horde of the post-war unemployed.

Inflation raged through Italy. The peacetime Kingdom of Italy was half graveyard and half clearing-sale.

Secondari spoke to people of influence in Turin, hoping to find something worthy to do with himself. Sadly, no one in Turin could recognize his superhuman qualities. Once they learned that he had died in battle, the people of Turin were perturbed. His own family doubted what he told them. They insulted him with their pity.

Angry scenes ensued—especially with his older brother. Secondari's older brother had never joined the Royal Army, being much too busy running the family enterprise of arms dealing. Those who fired the weapons did not prosper. Those who built the weapons had done well by the Great War.

Secondari came to realize that he despised his older brother. He loathed that placid, civilian charmer, already going to fat, with his boulevardier's mustache, his stickpin and tie, his gray gloves, and his eager, twinkling, lecherous eye for a factory girl.

He could not stay in a city that would shelter such a man. He would have to find a holocaust city, a place fit for himself.

III
OCCUPIED FIUME, 1919–1920

THE CITY OF
Fiume was a martyr
to the world's peace.

Fiume had long been an Austro-Hungarian seaport: a subjection that the locals always resented. When Austria-Hungary shattered to bits, the large Italian faction of the population naturally expected to become part of Italy.

The League of Nations had frustrated this natural hope. Instead, the peacemakers callously donated Fiume to the new, unheard-of Kingdom of Yugoslavia.

In her anguish and her shame, Fiume cried out for heroes—men of vision, who would save imperilled Fiume from the evil machinations of American President Woodrow Wilson.

The city's cry of pain was heard. Saviors arrived in a convoy of stolen Italian military trucks.

On September 12, 1919—a date as important as that of any great battle of the Great War—the Italian rebels had "deserted forward into the Future," and invaded Fiume. The people of Fiume showered the soldiers with roses in the palmy streets.

The Prophet, the Seven of Ronchi, and the Ace of Hearts. These uniformed Futurist Overmen were the avant-garde of the Twentieth Century. These were the visionaries, the men willing to defy the whole world to see justice done for one town.

Lorenzo Secondari had limped and wobbled into Fiume about a month later. Like many other Fiume adventurers, he had arrived uninvited, unknown, hungry, and penniless.

The "Desperates" were the wretched and the lost. These young men arrived in Fiume from all over war-stricken Italy. The Desperates came from anywhere where life was hard, but honor was still bright.

Because of Secondari's deafness, he had quickly blundered into a meaningless quarrel with a fellow, bewildered Desperate. He and his foe were on the point of a pistol duel, when the Prophet had personally intervened.

The Prophet had saved Secondari because the Prophet tenderly cherished every Desperate who joined his cause. Being a great poet, the Prophet saw deep into the souls of everyone he met—men, and especially women.

So the Prophet gazed, with his one remaining good eye, into Secondari's two eyes. Then he reached up with his gray-gloved hand. He tenderly touched the stub of Secondari's blasted ear.

In that intimate encounter, the Prophet had seen all and forgiven all.

Aware that Secondari could not properly hear his words of wisdom, the Prophet had written Secondari a personal letter. This ardent, fatherly missive was boldly scrawled across three pages of the Prophet's personal stationery. Each precious page featured a stamped Latin motto, and a handsome woodcut of an Arditi dagger ripping the League of Nations to shreds.

The Prophet's letter was a generous gift to a troubled, wounded soldier. Frank, terse, and manly, this letter was a transformational screed. The letter made it clear to Secondari that he had a Cause: the Future—and a role to play: the creation of a pirate utopia.

As a further act of generosity, the Prophet had also sent Secondari the gift of a personal diary. The Prophet urged the troubled soldier to set down his Futuristic thoughts and plans. This writerly effort would allow Secondari to transcend his youthful confusion and mature into a man of destiny.

Designed in Milan to commemorate the Prophet's war-time "Flight over Vienna," this blank tome was a magnificent feat of "Liberty Style" design craft, its sumptuous leather cover embossed with mystical stars and sinuous silver trees.

Nestled inside the Torpedo Factory, night by lonely night, Secondari poured his soul into those diary pages.

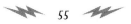

Secondari tried to write something worthy of himself each night, because Revolutionary Fiume, the "Holocaust City," the "River Inexhaustible," was a city of writers.

Revolutionary Fiume thronged with literary men-at-arms. Writers, first and foremost, had answered the clarion call of the great warrior-poet. Before the Future could exist, the Future had to be written into being.

The Prophet himself was the first and foremost among all these armed writers, of course. But the glistening black flame of his Fiuman cause had attracted many high-spirited men of the pen: Marinetti, Vecchi, Pedrazzi, Carli, Susmi, Mazzucatto, Miani, Coselchi… Valiant foreign writers had also joined the Prophet's crusade, the American Henry Furst, the Belgian Léon Kochnitzky. Other writers were sure to follow.

When Secondari gazed back over his badly spelled diary entries, he knew that he was not a writer. He was an engineer. Nevertheless, Secondari was amazed by the speed and depth of his own spiritual advancement. Living in Fiume, and entirely conscious of the daily life of Revolution, he was even more Fiuman than the writers were. He had become the pirate engineer among the pirate writers. The molten iron of his discontent had become a cold blue steel.

THE ACE OF HEARTS

was a lion: broad of chest,
thick of arm. He dressed entirely
in black military gear, and had long,
cascading hair and a bristling mustache
and beard. The Ace of Hearts had the light,
glowing eyes of a predatory beast.

The Ace of Hearts was a Milanese aristocrat, and also a combat air ace. The Ace was the
Prophet's right-hand man. He brought into being
what the Prophet merely foresaw.

The Ace of Hearts was a renowned expert in aerial
reconnaissance. Outside Fiume, the Ace had built himself a secret viewing platform, camouflaged high within
an oak tree's mighty branches.

This secret, clifftop treehouse gave the Ace a full, stra-
tegic overview of the Fiume harbor. From his tree, he could

arget-spot any incoming planes or possible attack boats. He could see anyone, in short, who might care to spoil the weapons-test that was taking place down at sea level.

The Ace and Secondari settled into the secret tree-house with a radio set and field binoculars. The Ace had a little stove and a coffee-pot within his treehouse, and a small, select library of Futurist poetry, and even a handy chamber-pot.

In the pirate utopia of Fiume, the Ace of Hearts was the greatest utopian pirate of all. He was the spymaster, the lord of secrets. The Ace of Hearts was a bandit artist. He broke civilized rules that lesser men could not dream of breaking.

During the Great War, the Ace of Hearts had killed thousands of men. He did this by conveying his splendid aerial photographs to Italian artillerymen, who had loaded and launched the shells.

Secondari and the Ace of Hearts were war comrades. This was why the two of them were not civilian participants in city politics, down on the stony beach. They were two warriors, covert and fanatical, perched above and beyond the politicians, with spotter binoculars and a field radio.

"In half an hour," said the Ace of Hearts, speaking slowly, clearly, and loudly, into Secondari's good ear, "we will see if this comedy of yours is your wedding, or my funeral."

"Oh, my warheads will detonate, sir," Secondari promised. "The trick in any modern torpedo is in the motors and the guidance. That tub out there lies at short range. We can't miss."

"If that hulk out there fails to blow sky-high," said the Ace, "Fiume will be the laughingstock of the world. Do you see all those foreign reporters down there? Those bastards will turn our great spiritual adventure into an Italian comic opera."

Secondari was entirely unconcerned. He had already tested the missiles. They were simple, workaday Austrian nautical torpedoes that his Torpedo Factory had been designed to build. The water-borne torpedoes were merely a necessary step toward his true dream of radio-controlled, airborne, Futurist torpedoes.

He had managed to restore the factory to working order, and built a short production run of the Great War's favorite nautical bombs.

He knew for a fact that his torpedoes really worked. Together with the Croat pirates—always his comrades in these ventures—he had quietly motored past the sea-mines that protected the Fiume harbor. They'd found a rusty wreck marooned on an obscure reef near the island of Veglia, launched torpedoes at it, and blown it to scrap.

"My torpedoes work," he said. "I don't care how many Americans are watching. Do you know how many people were watching when torpedoes sank the *Lusitania*? One thousand, nine hundred and fifty-nine."

The Ace of Hearts lowered his binoculars and stared.

"I understand that you recently stole an armored car, Lieutenant," he said. "I've given you some odd assignments. Stealing a tank wasn't one of them."

"I didn't steal a tank, just a Lancia-Ansaldo model

IZM," Secondari corrected. "Anyway, they were just some Communists."

"The Prophet would probably give you a medal for caning a Communist."

"What, one of his own medals?" said Secondari. "Or one of his own Communists?"

The Ace of Hearts considered this quip. His bearded lips twitched, but he had never been known to laugh aloud. "Was that a risky political joke, Lorenzo? I didn't know that you Turinese had that in you."

He passed his binoculars to Secondari.

Down on a steep and stony cove east of the city harbor, some wooden bleachers had been erected. Fringed with pines, the stony little theater faced the sea. Out there in the sparkling Adriatic, a worthless old barge had been mocked-up with balsa-wood and cardboard. It looked something like a battleship—maybe an Austrian Imperial battleship, or maybe a British or American battleship... It could be anybody's battleship, because torpedoes weren't choosy about the ships they blew to hell.

The Prophet was presiding over this display. The foreign press corps was in attendance. Many of them had newsreel cameras. The foreign press adored the Prophet. His works were vividly newsworthy.

It was certainly worthy world news if the Prophet's "Regency of Carnaro" could successfully manufacture naval torpedoes. Any properly made torpedo could sink any battleship. With a fleet of fast, piratical speedboats equipped with working torpedoes, the tiny Regency of Carnaro could hold the whole Adriatic hostage. After all, during the Great War, German U-boats with torpedoes had done precisely the same thing to the Atlantic Ocean.

And, given that reality: imagine torpedoes that flew effortlessly over both land and water, and were guided to their targets by invisible, unerring radio beams. What would the world of tomorrow make of that invention?

Down at the stony beach, a self-propelled howitzer tractor, adorned with roses and Latin slogans, tracked its weapons past the witnesses.

A crew of Revolutionary sailors dismounted the torpedoes from their wooden sledge. They rolled the long metallic cylinders, with many ceremonial flourishes, onto a flower-strewn pontoon dock. These sailors wore brand-new Regency of Carnaro uniforms—blue, white, and very angular, like costumes for aquatic harlequins.

The gleaming torpedoes were tenderly lowered into the glistening sea, then dashed with flutes of champagne. The sailors shouted a poetic war-cry. A crackling bugle fanfare sounded from the pole-mounted gramophone loudspeakers.

Secondari scanned the crowd with his field-glasses. He was searching the crowd for his enemies. Because he had made real torpedoes, he had also made real enemies. He exulted in having these enemies.

Because it was a Balkan city, the city of Fiume abounded in inimical factions—more so even than a typical Italian city.

The Prophet was the city's Commandant, the military Dictator of Fiume, its guiding light and great orator.

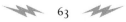

However, the Prophet could not protect Secondari from the scheming of the lesser men within his city.

The Mayor of Fiume was in attendance at the weapons test, along with his entire elected city council. The city councilors of Fiume were, without exception, prosperous and evil men.

The middle-aged leaders of the "Young Fiume" radicals had arrived within the bleachers. The "Sedi Riuniti" Socialist labor union, too. The Fiume Autonomist Party. The Chamber of Labor. The Apostolic Administrator of the Roman Catholic Church....

Such a small crowd of people, yet such a grand, tumultuous, many-sided struggle. In Fiume, there were more great world causes to fight about than there were men to represent them.

Frau Piffer was among all these quarrelsome, Balkanized men. Being a woman, she made a startling figure among all the beards, top-hats, and military brass. Frau Piffer wore the dream-like, unlikely dress of a Carnaro Corporate Syndicalist. She looked like a daffodil on a coal-heap.

Frau Piffer had also brought her child to witness the glorious event: little Maria Piffer, who was dressed in a blue-striped sailor-suit and a ribboned straw hat.

Secondari sharpened the focus of his field-glasses. Maria Piffer was the only native of Fiume that Secondari entirely understood. Secondari was deaf, while Maria Piffer scarcely spoke any Italian. The two of them didn't talk much together. Nevertheless, he and Maria Piffer had become spiritual intimates. They had really found a bond.

Maria Piffer was a true native child of the Twentieth Century. Maria was entirely at her ease inside a weapons factory. Being seven years old, Maria Piffer hated schools. She despised and feared churches.

Secondari had even seen Maria Piffer stealing and hiding small, shiny objects from the Torpedo Factory, so that she could keep them for herself. He found this action entirely endearing. He went out of his way to see to it that she got away with doing it.

In the solemn pews of the wooden bleachers, among the worthy local statesmen, the little pirate child was itchy, restless, and unappeasable.

Secondari hated his enemies with a wide and generous hatred. In looking them over, he also realized that he didn't much care for his friends. But Maria Piffer was not like that. She was not of their time, among them but just not one of them.

He loved Maria Piffer. He wanted her to grow and to thrive.

If torpedoes blew up everyone on the high seas—if flying bombs blew up everyone in the world—Maria Piffer was the only person he would miss. She was the only one whose grave would leave a hole within him.

The target barge exploded. Wet fireworks of Adriatic spume flew in every direction. Promptly, the barge exploded a second time. Tall flames jetted hither and yon, and uprising clouds of steam mixed with the plummeting foam. The shattered barge exploded a third time, cracking in half in an orgiastic tumble of shattering, sinking iron.

The Ace of Hearts methodically scanned the sea and sky for any signs of enemy intervention.

Secondari rubbed at his right jawbone. The shock wave from the distant bombs had cracked something loose within the ruins of his right ear. He seemed to mystically sense, more than truly hear, the tickling sensation. But his dead ear had, somehow, come back to life.

"I could swear that I heard three explosions," he said.

"That third burst was mine," said the Ace of Hearts. "I hid two kilos of dynamite inside that hulk, in case your torpedoes were duds."

"That is very like you," said Secondari.

The Ace of Hearts shrugged his mighty shoulders. "If our great enterprise fails here in Fiume, I'll have to leave for South America. I wouldn't much care for a future like that."

Secondari scanned the beach with his binoculars. The exulting crowd was recovering their posh, expensive hats, after tossing them in the air. Maria Piffer had escaped her mother's control during the bursting explosions. The little girl was frolicking alone behind the bleachers.

"Well," said Secondari. "That made the headlines for us. And now?"

"Now," said the Ace of Hearts, "it's time that we settle our accounts with the local bourgeoisie down there. Look at those civilian sons of bitches, pretending enthusiasm for your noble feat of arms."

"Vico, Gigante, Grossich, Maylander, and Zanella," Secondari recited. The Ace of Hearts had compiled a handy list of their mutual enemies.

"Our opponents resent our spiritual greatness and our freedom of action," said the Ace of Hearts. "They envy us. Once they were great men of property and principle, here in Fiume. These local magnates make it their business to impair our path to destiny."

"We have won the War of the Titans," said Secondari. "We won't fail at this war of the pygmies."

"I was pleased," said the Ace of Hearts thoughtfully, "when Signor Vico, the owner of your Torpedo Factory, fled Fiume and ran to Zurich."

"When you recruited me, sir," said Secondari, "you told me that I was a desperate pirate. You promised me dirty work. Well, my Croats and I—we grabbed Vico. We smacked him around, shaved his head, and threw him out of town. My only regret is that I didn't put six bullets through him."

"Lorenzo, what can we do about those worthless people of decency? There are always so many more of them than there are visionaries like us!"

"Do you really want my advice, sir?"

"Well, yes I do, Lorenzo. I can see by your face that you need to speak that out."

"I have a solution for us. But it's not work for lawyers. Or bankers, or poets, or philosophers. It's an engineering solution."

"Let me hear of it."

Secondari pointed north, through the leafy branches of the oak tree, to the rugged castle hill that dominated the city. "Set mortars up there, onto target grids. Shell their mansions before dawn. Catch them all sleeping, with their

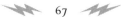

wives, kids, and kitty-cats. Blow those sons of bitches right off the map!"

The Ace of Hearts contemplated this proposal. "Well, you and I could certainly do that."

"We did that every day, during the war! I know: in peacetime, maybe that sounds 'dishonorable.' Well, that's all just talk! The law means nothing but words on paper. The Croats and I are willing to carry it out!"

"Are you sure you can do it?"

"Of course! They are very good pirates, these Balkan people. My pirates aren't fat gentlemen! They're not bankers on a city council! They're the *ustashe*, they're the *uscocchi*, they are true Balkan pirates! So—once they've done what's necessary here in Fiume, just give them a rifle, and a good horse, and fill their rotten teeth with gold! Send them back to their villages! They'll be fine."

The Ace of Hearts thoughtfully stroked his beard.

"As for me, sir," said Secondari, "forge me another passport. Then I'm off to America. I can speak English. I don't mind exile. Goodbye and good luck. Your political problem here in Fiume will be over, it will exist no more. No people, no problem."

"You have made me a generous offer," said the Ace of Hearts. "That is typical of you."

"'I possess what I give away.' That's what the Prophet always says to us, isn't it? Well, fine! I will give myself away for our great Cause of Fiume. I'm willing to do it—if you kill the ruling class! Erase them! Liquidate them without pity. Build the new world on their bones! It's the only way to make anything that's fresh and clean! Do it! Then the Future is really yours. Otherwise, never!"

The Ace of Hearts gazed at him for many heartbeats, without speaking. "Your logic is clear, my friend. However: our Commandant would prefer a more elegant, suave approach to creating a world fit for heroes."

"I knew you would say that!" Secondari shouted. "That is gallantry, that's not a Revolution! I offered you a final solution! You'll be sorry."

"I have heard your offer and I am telling you, 'no!'" the Ace bellowed. "A man with your skill and commitment is far too valuable for that! You're my pirate engineer, you're my best military asset! I can't throw a man like you away for the sake of killing five fat civilian idiots in this little town! A man with your ability should be building amazing Futurist weapons, fit to terrify the whole world!"

The Ace pulled a lacquered box of drugs from under his poetry bookcase. Using a brass trench lighter, the Ace of Hearts lit a brown Turkish-leaf cigarette. He passed it to Secondari, then lit another for himself.

"No more politics from you, all right?" said the Ace of Hearts, blowing smoke. "Your demonstration here was a great success! Your Anarcho-Syndicalist factory has built a native product, right here in Fiume, the whole world will be forced to respect! I congratulate you."

Secondari saluted, from where he sat cross-legged on the boards of the secret treehouse. "Thank you, sir."

"So, let's talk practically, eh? Let's talk about the future of your factory. What new resources do you need from your

government? This is the moment to ask me for favors. Be frank."

"All right. Give me command over every other industrial factory in this city. I want control of the tobacco factory, the paper factory, the shipyards, and the oil refinery, too. I'll Syndicalize every one of them. I'll kick out every fat bloodsucker who holds us back, with all their stupid laws and legal regulations. All the means of production must go directly to the pirate engineers."

The Ace of Hearts narrowed his pale eyes. "So. This is your mistress, the Communist, who is talking to me now."

"No, no, that's not true at all! Frau Piffer is not my mistress! I don't need a woman, I have no time for one. I only have time for the Future."

The Ace of Hearts raised his hairy brows. "Are you truly that dogmatic? Are you a monk? Our Fiume Revolution is a Revolution of Love! Our Revolution is a great world rebellion about Youth, Love, and Music. That's what makes our Prophet's cause entirely different from all other revolutions."

Secondari did not care to contradict the political doctrines of the Prophet. A poet with a thousand mistresses was an Overman. "Well," he said, "I admit it, I have no mistress at the moment. If I did, then she wouldn't be a woman like Frau Piffer."

"Oh, come on, why not give it a whirl? Everyone in Fiume knows that she adores you. To conquer a woman is dangerous—but to scorn a woman is worse."

"No woman is a technical solution, that's why! I'm a pirate engineer! I don't want a girlfriend, I want a revolution in popular mechanics! We need real factories that can work! We can't just lift the skirts of pretty girls, after we give them votes, and hashish, and jazz records!"

"Whatever does it take to please you, Lieutenant? I've never once seen you look happy. I worry about you. The Prophet must be thrilled about your new torpedoes now. He will let you name your own reward in Fiume. Isn't that enough?"

"I hate all these useless, beautiful gestures!" Secondari shouted. "The Prophet is a poet! He can't build industries with his sonnets! No matter what reward a poet may give me, those rich bourgeois louts with their ballot boxes, they'll just grab it all back! Capitalism must be smashed."

The Ace of Hearts said nothing. He gave the sky a last careful scan, including the zenith, and all three hundred and sixty degrees of the horizon.

Then he silently climbed down from the observation platform in the oak tree. Secondari followed him.

"You are not an easy man to please," the Ace of Hearts remarked at last. "I have tried to help you. I contacted those two professors you mentioned, in Turin. Those engineers, the two men who invented that Italian flying torpedo. They answered me, too—but they set me impossible conditions. They want stock ownership, and their own corporation. Also, they want to register their patents inside Britain and the USA. We can't do that. The USA is our enemy."

"They're engineers, but they're also cowards," said Secondari. "Did they tell you that they are loyal to the Kingdom of Italy, and the House of Savoy? My brother always preaches that rubbish."

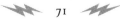

"They made a few such patriotic noises in their confidential letters, yes."

"To hell with the King's engineers. We'll send our own agents to Turin, sir. We will steal their plans and blueprints. We will pirate the flying torpedo. We'll build hundreds of them. Pirate torpedoes, with no legal rights, no patents, no permissions, and no mercy asked or given! Let them come here and try to sue us in our own courts. Ha! Those cowards wouldn't dare."

The Ace of Hearts brightened. "I believe I can help you with that plan. I like the sound of all that. That's how we've done things here from our very first day."

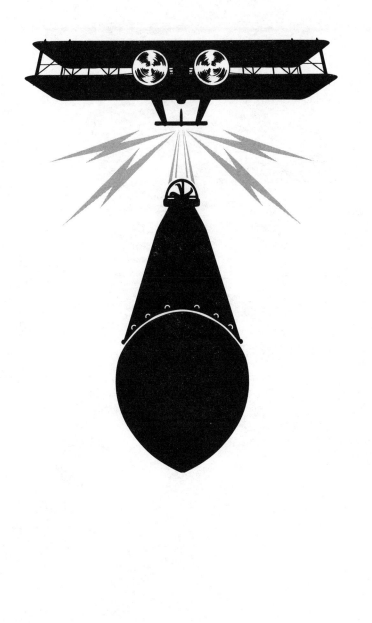

3: THE BRAVE NEW WORLD

v

THE REGENCY OF CARNARO, FEBRUARY 4, 1920

THE FACTORY GIRLS

naturally had to celebrate
their great success with the torpedoes. Ceremonial festivities were
conducted in the factory all day. Secondari was forced to participate in these rituals.
He also had to wear his new, Syndicalist, Regency of Carnaro uniform, which he disliked.

A great many medals and ribbons were distributed. As a special sign of his favor, the Prophet sent
along his mistress, the Pianist, to perform a concert
within the factory. Much valuable production time was
lost as the Pianist tinkled her way through the works of
Claude Debussy.

After her concert, the Pianist left her instrument and
harangued the factory girls. The Pianist was a ferocious
Venetian patriot. She swore a blood-oath that every scrap

of land ever owned by the historic Republic of Venice would be seized and redeemed to Venetian control.

Since the Republic of Venice had once owned Crete, Cyprus, and large parts of Turkey and Bulgaria, this was a land-grab to surprise even the wildest Italian patriot.

The factory girls gave the Pianist a generous round of applause because she was a fine lady. They also admired the Pianist's willingness to flout convention. She was a classical musician openly living as the concubine of a married poet. In this way, the First Lady of Carnaro was visibly living the dream.

The Constitutionalist also took care to appear at the festivities. Carnaro's greatest political theorist made no formal speech, but he simply mixed, in his friendly, persuasive fashion, directly with the workers.

The Constitutionalist registered the workers to vote, and he explained to them that their Syndicate owned the factory. He told the working women that their factory was in the avant-garde of all world factories.

In the Regency of Carnaro, property would be owned by those who made the best use of property. Absentee financial ownership of factories would be entirely illegal. Only those who ran the means of production would own it.

Under the ingenious Constitution of the Regency of Carnaro, the ownership of property was determined entirely by judgements of its use-value. The State was divided into ten Corporations—including a Tenth Corporation of Supermen.

These ten republican corporations would jointly guide civil society, in a harmonious method, akin to the various sections of an orchestra.

The franchise was universal for all citizens of Carnaro, regardless of their race, creed, ethnicity, or color. Women had completely equal political rights, with equal pay as well. Unemployment was banished by decree. Fulfilling work in an atmosphere of beauty and creativity was guaranteed to all.

The women of the Torpedo Factory were excited to learn that they were leaders of such worldwide significance. Several women workers solemnly swore to move into the factory around the clock, and live there, and eat there, and sleep in there, until production levels were doubled.

Frau Piffer was overjoyed by this flow of pride and good spirits within her establishment. She was radiant and thriving, but Secondari found the crowd stifling. Ceremonies always bored him, and his right ear, newly restored to life, was itching and panging him.

Secondari was preparing to flee when an unforeseen event occurred. A young military engineer came to him to shyly offer his own services.

The new recruit was a radio engineer, a Genoese war veteran named Giulio Ulivi. Ulivi had witnessed the torpedo demonstration.

Ulivi said that he had been conducting some private radio experiments in the amateur tradition of Marconi. During these amateur efforts, Ulivi had discovered a new form of radiation, the "F-Ray."

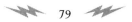

Ulivi claimed that his invisible F-Ray, when properly focussed and aimed, had military potential. He'd killed some rabbits and mice with his F-Ray apparatus at his mother's house.

Ulivi had patriotically offered his discovery to the Italian War Ministry. The short-sighted bureaucrats had rejected his generous offer, though, and even insulted him.

Secondari could not understand half of the excited ramble of this Genoese technician. However, his deafness had taught him to read expressions. Secondari therefore knew, within a matter of moments, that Ulivi was entirely honest and sincere. He was intelligent and rational, as well.

However, the Genoese engineer was hopelessly misled by an extraordinary obsession.

Secondari was kind to Ulivi. He made him welcome. He promised him food, shelter, political protection, and a career of important work on the radio-guidance of flying torpedoes.

The sudden appearance of Giulio Ulivi was like the first flower in spring. In the future, there would be many bright young men, just like Ulivi, arriving in Carnaro. The Regency of Carnaro was growing powerful, and there would be consequences in this.

He, Secondari, would have to organize these eager men, and set them into the course of useful work, and become their patron. He would have to be, not just a pirate engineer, but the boss of pirate engineers.

This matter distinguished the work of engineers from the work of poets. Successful mass production needed scale,

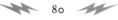

it needed hierarchy. Understanding this, Secondari retreated, to confront his own thoughts in his diary.

Secondari had built himself a snug private barracks within the Torpedo Factory. He lived within a windowless store-room. This bomb-shelter was sturdily blastproofed, through the battlefield expedient of lining walls, floor, and roof with thick, crisscrossed sets of steel railroad ties.

In his six-sided steel bomb-shelter, Secondari slept in safety. He passed each night on his military trestle-cot, with its four wooden legs set into four pannikins of kerosene. This trench-warfare trick kept any rats, lice, or bedbugs at bay.

His secured shelter had toolboxes, water canteens, canned rations, pistol ammunition, a sturdy kerosene lantern, and thick stacks of popular science magazines, most of them in English.

The shelter was silent, secured and restful, and once he'd barred the steel door with two heavy fragments of railroad tie, he was left alone, to think and strategize. Alone, in the golden lamplight, with only the pure, strange music of his damaged ears for company.

VI
THE REGENCY OF CARNARO, FEBRUARY 5, 1920

TWO DAYS AFTER

the torpedo demonstra-
tion, the Ace of Hearts sent
a courier to the Torpedo Factory,
demanding Secondari's immediate attendance at the Hotel Europa.

The Hotel Europa was the best hotel in
the city of Fiume, and therefore the water-
ing hole of the Italian rebel officer corps. The
Prophet and his writerly staff worked inside the
Fiume City Hall. The Ace had chosen the Hotel
Europa for the regime's covert and underground
activities.

The Ace of Hearts received Secondari in a pent-
house suite at the Europa. The suite was littered with
operational maps, glistening aerial photos, and framed,
signed photos of pretty French actresses.

The Ace of Hearts closed and locked his mahogany office door. He checked all the windows, shuttered them, and took his white telephone off its shining brass hook.

"Secret news has just arrived, of vital importance," said the Ace of Hearts. "Some news is good, while some is bad. Which intelligence would you like to learn first?"

Secondari rolled up a leather chair on its castors, cupped his hand to his good ear, and leaned across the desk. "Tell me the bad news."

"Fiume has lost one of our best allies. There was an armed attack yesterday in the offices of the Milanese newspaper, *People of Italy* (*Popolo d'Italia*). The editor was one of our boldest friends."

Secondari struggled with his instant surge of outrage. "Ha! So! Attacking our writers, is it? To stifle our voices of justice! The Communists, I suppose! Those cowards burn one of our newspapers? Well, we'll burn five of theirs!"

"It was the editor's ex-wife who shot him, actually," said the Ace of Hearts. "Or she was his mistress, anyway. Some creature he was involved with, before his regular church marriage. You know the irregular lives of these newspaper men… Anyway, this mad wife of his brought along a female accomplice, a Futurist cabaret dancer. These two pretty girls sweet-talked their way into the newspaper office. Then they pulled pistols out of their purses, and they opened fire on our man."

"Women," said Secondari.

"Small caliber, single-shot pistols," said the Ace of Hearts. "They hit him twice. Mussolini's not dead—but they aimed right at the area where a man least likes to be shot."

"So, our Mussolini's been shot, eh? Too bad, I liked Mussolini! A brave man, hit by a cannon shell on the front—I know what that's like! To think that he'd survive the Great War, and then be shot down by two pretty girls! What a bordello of a country Italy is, for God's sake! Always some dirty scandal."

"They caught the wife. The cops have locked her up," said the Ace of Hearts. "She's a madwoman, she's raving her head off. That Futurist girl, though, she escaped the police in Milan. She's a clever, dangerous woman. She fled to Egypt, my agents tell me."

"Marinetti is from Egypt," said Secondari. "She knows Marinetti, being a Futurist?"

"Oh, yes. And Egypt is in full rebellion now, against the British Empire. So Cairo makes a splendid place for a Futurist dancing girl to hide from authorities. Our little fugitive is Valentine de Saint-Point, the author of the *Manifesto of Futurist Lust*. Did you ever read that?"

"No."

"You should read it. It's excellent."

"She's some lustful, Futurist, dancing girl in Egypt, yet she's also a published writer?"

The Ace of Hearts nodded. "She can write. She's great. I can't say that I blame her, really. What is a free woman of spirit to do—about a tactless cad like Mussolini? You never see any women shooting at our Prophet, although he's had a thousand women."

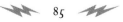

"Well, we can always get ourselves another newspaper editor," said Secondari. "The world is full of writers who want to be editors. Just pick another one! Our Cause marches on."

The Ace of Hearts leaned back in his leather office chair, and laced his hands through his mass of tangled hair. "Mussolini lacked any proper taste in literature, anyway. He's a typical village Socialist. Did you see that silly emblem that Mussolini foisted on our Movement?"

"That old axe with the sticks tied to it?" said Secondari. "I hated that axe! You can't *use* an axe with sticks tangled all over it! We're all Futurists now! That ancient Roman fascist axe is two thousand years old!"

"You seem rather angry about Signor Mussolini, Lorenzo," the Ace of Hearts observed. "I don't suppose you had some personal quarrel with Mussolini? Those women who shot Mussolini—they used some pistols that were made right here in your factory."

"I don't get angry, sir." Secondari patted the new Beretta mounted on his hip. "Because I'm a man of cold-blooded logic. That's why. If I'd shot Mussolini, he'd have five rounds from this! One in the gut, three in the heart, and one through the head."

The Ace of Hearts pursed his bearded lips. "I'm going to tell you the good news, now."

Secondari leaned forward in taut anticipation. Ooze flowed from his right ear.

"This is good news about our very worst enemy," said the Ace of Hearts. "I mean President Woodrow Wilson, the

tyrant of the League of Nations. Woodrow Wilson has had a stroke. He's paralyzed. He's crippled in his brain. Wilson is even worse off than our own Mussolini—and Mussolini is ruined for life."

"So, was it the Communists?" said Secondari.

"We do suspect the Communists, yes. Wilson fell ill during the Paris Peace Talks. Likely, Woodrow Wilson fell on the very same evil day when he gave Fiume away to the Yugoslavs."

Secondari shook his head. The stump of his right ear was tingling. "Oh, well, I just don't believe that news, sir. That news is too good to be true. Isn't that wishful thinking?"

"I know, it does sound fantastic—but I also know that it's true. The President's habits, his daily activities, they've all changed since that injustice that he did to Fiume. I've kept a careful dossier. I have many different sources. Wilson is finished."

"Well, then I hope it really was poison," said Secondari. "I'd love to shake the hand of the man who poisoned Woodrow Wilson. I don't care if he's a Communist, or a black magician. After what he did, he is one of us."

"We may never know what struck Wilson down, but we do know that the American President is an imbecile. The American government is now being run through Wilson's aide-de-camp. Colonel House is his name. Wilson's equerry is a Texan gentleman, he's an Army cavalier. A fighting man, like us."

"Wait, be careful, sir," said Secondari. "This is too good. This must be a trap, sir. It's some American trick."

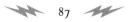

The Ace of Hearts drew a deep, satisfied breath. "The truth is: Woodrow Wilson was always an imbecile! That stupid American professor—he meddled in Europe, and the Swedes gave him the Nobel Peace Prize for that—well, Wilson has met the fate he fully earned! He's a wreck now, a ruin! But this Colonel House fellow, this Texan cavalryman—he's a man we can understand."

Secondari began to tremble in his chair. "Please speak more slowly, sir."

"I'll let you savor it. You see: Colonel House is one of us—in his own Texan way, of course. The Prophet wrote to Colonel House secretly, to that effect. The Prophet wrote him a wonderful letter, eloquent, persuasive, one of his best! And—just yesterday—we have received a secret reply from Colonel House. House wants to negotiate with us."

"Your good news is amazing, sir!" said Secondari, his heart hammering in his chest. "It's as if—in one moment—we were suddenly living in a different world!"

"Yes, we are. The world of the League of Nations is doomed," said the Ace of Hearts. "Without President Wilson to push his crazy scheme, his own Congress won't vote for the League of Nations! The American people will defy their own tyrant and refuse to the join the League! Because the Americans want to be free, just like we do!"

Secondari felt a pang deep within his ear. Dizziness seized him and the world spun around him. He almost fell from his swivel chair.

"We're winning!" he shouted. "I always believed we

would win—but my God, we really are winning! I don't have to believe any more, because it's the truth!"

"Colonel House is sending us agents from the United States Secret Service. American spies are coming here. They want to discuss the suppression of Communism and also our local oil refinery." The Ace allowed himself a predatory smile. "And the Yankees want to talk to us about your naval torpedoes, of course. That's why I've called you in here. You are our expert in arms proliferation."

"Hurry! Quick! Give the American spies whatever they want!" Secondari cried. He struggled to rise, became even dizzier. "Give them wine, women, opera songs! Forgive me for weeping, sir! I can't help myself, I'm so happy."

"My 'good news' is quite shocking, isn't it?" said the Ace of Hearts. "Until yesterday, the Americans were our worst enemies. Now, imagine the Yankees as our friends, eh? The Balkans will be at our feet."

Secondari sat upright. The news about the wreck of the League of Nations had lifted the weight of the whole world from his bones. "This is Great Power politics at work. Any Italian child would know what to do next!"

The Ace of Hearts helped him to his feet. "What would you advise me to do, Secondari?"

"Isn't it obvious?"

"Well, I know what our regime has in mind, of course. I just wonder what you, as a pirate engineer, think Carnaro should do."

"We lead the way into the Future, of course! With industry, with engineering—and from a real position of strength! Marinetti is entirely right. Out with the old Roman statues. Now we bring in the race cars."

"That old man, who is our Prophet," said the Ace of Hearts, "wants us to march to Zagreb at once, to destroy Yugoslavia. He wants to attack and invade the Balkans, as soon as we can."

"Of course. He's an audacious hero, he always wants to attack at once! But how? With what artillery, what battle tanks, what aircraft, what lines of supply? We have to build all that."

"The Prophet plans to use Italian arms. In order to conquer the Balkans, from here in Fiume, we'll have to march on Rome first. We will dissolve the Parliament, depose the present King, then make the Prophet the Commandant of Italy. That's the great dream of Carnaro."

"Oh, stop talking such balls! That's an epic poem! That's not a military strategy! Where would we get the gasoline for our trucks, for our tanks? We don't have one working oil refinery in Fiume! We can't just ride into Rome on horseback, yelling beautiful speeches!"

"That worked for Garibaldi."

"No it didn't! Not at all! Garibaldi became a crippled old man, stuck alone on some tiny island! Do you want that life of exile to happen to our Prophet? This is the Twentieth Century! We'll never seize the Future by singing poems, with a guitar, from some gondola! Do we want a future Italy that's some museum of antiquities? Italy, overrun with foreign honeymooners?"

"No, that's not the future I desire for Italy," said the Ace of Hearts. "That is a very dark future. I didn't risk my life a hundred times aloft, for any future like that. Can you save us from that fate, Lieutenant? How?"

Secondari struggled to control himself. He did not care to argue politics with the Ace of Hearts. He knew that he was outmatched.

Secondari deeply respected, and even loved, the Ace of Hearts. He had often tried—and failed—to emulate the Ace's paradoxical mix of cool, sporting indolence with ruthless revolutionary fervor. Even a Nietzschean Overman could never possess such Milanese suavity as the Ace of Hearts.

The Ace of Hearts was the Fiume Revolution's true genius. Because the Ace of Hearts was a living bomb of Twentieth Century radicalism. The Ace had shot down six aircraft in mortal combat, and yet he was a Mason, a mystic, a yogi, and a nudist; a forger, a wiretapper, a partaker of cocaine and marijuana; a philosophical anarchist with a superb devotion to music and free love. The Ace of Hearts was the finest man that Secondari had ever encountered.

In the stress of the moment, however, Secondari realized that he and the Ace had to find some way to meet as equal spirits. The Ace was a liberation mystic while Secondari was merely an engineer, but they were also two suffering human beings within the maelstrom of a profound political struggle. They had to transcend the limitations of their roles. They had to find a way to make Futurism work.

"Well," said Secondari to the Ace, "tell me something. What do *you* want? You asked me what I wanted. What about yourself?"

"Since you ask me," said the Ace slowly, "I will open my heart to you. What I want is to go big-game hunting. Maybe a lion in Ethiopia. Or else some sweet-tempered countess in Paris. But my desires are not my duty. After today's developments, my future is clear to me. I'm to become the Minister of State Security for an Anarcho-Syndicalist government."

Secondari was silenced by this firm answer. It was dutiful, it was direct, it had the sound of solidity and sense. He didn't know what to say to it. He, Lorenzo Secondari, was only twenty-four years old, while the Ace of Hearts was all of twenty-seven. The Ace had the advantage of maturity.

"At my tailors' in Milan, they're already stitching my new uniform," said the Ace somberly. "And as for you, my friend, well, you should also join my government. I have a role for you, and a title: the 'Pirate Engineer.' No, wait—no, the foreign press will never understand that terminology.... That title doesn't suit a man like you, it's not scary enough.... I have it! You will be our 'Minister of Vengeance Weapons.'"

VII
THE REGENCY OF CARNARO,
FEBRUARY 14, 1920–
MAY 1, 1920

AS AN OFFICIAL

Minister within the
government of the Regency
of Carnaro, Secondari had to bid a
farewell to his beloved Torpedo Factory.
State politics required him to move into the
Hotel Europa, the den of the Carnaro elite.

Secondari soon discovered that the Hotel
Europa was a seething Futurist orgy. The elite of
Carnaro were loyal disciples of their Prophet, a poet
who kept a harem.

By his previous, decadent standards—for he was an
Italian poet who had known the intimate favors of a thousand women—the Prophet's harem in Fiume was quite
small and efficient. He had only five women available.

The Pianist was the Prophet's titular mistress. She was a
Venetian musician one-third his age. He was also visited by

the Art Witch, a rich Milanese aristocrat who entertained the Prophet with her black masses and spiritual séances.

His female secretary, and his female housekeeper, waited on the Prophet by day, and also by night. The Prophet's legal wife sometimes appeared in Fiume, for form's sake.

Taking their cue from these habits of their supremo, the soldiers of Carnaro freed themselves from the strictures of pre-war propriety. They were love warriors and love revolutionaries: nudists, kama-yogis, and homosexuals. In the Hotel Europa, suites were reserved for the free-love soirees of multiple partners.

Oddly, very few of the women of Fiume seemed at all upset or surprised by this aspect of their Revolution. The women of Fiume simply drank in the Prophet's honeyed words, much like the thousand women he had already seduced. The women of Fiume even seemed flattered by the trust he put in them. He had given them the vote, equal legal rights, and equal pay for equal work.

So the women of Fiume started businesses. They attended book clubs for women, and studied law and medicine, and even engineering. They ran for political offices, and became aviatrixes and radio talk-show hostesses. They were proud to be pioneering free women of the Twentieth Century.

As a regime administrator, Secondari came to understand the doctrines of Constitutional Anarcho-Syndicalism. Under Anarcho-Syndicalism, financial ownership was banned by state decree. Private property could only be owned by syndicates of laborers. In short, Syndicalism meant taking everything from the rich, and giving everything to the technocrats and their work-forces.

As a Carnaro Corporate Syndicalist, Lorenzo Secondari remained a Pirate Engineer. But he no longer stole from the poorly guarded military depots of the Great War. Instead, his new task as a government official was to steal the country from the legal control of the rich, and give it to the labor force.

This radical act of social revolution was a dirty job. Secondari did his duty with gusto. He did not hesitate to bring the war straight to the doors of the rich. He and his men came in pre-dawn squadron attacks. They had trucks, pistols, clubs, and rifles. They cut wire fences, they shattered locks, they broke bones, they burned doors. They seized booty and abducted prisoners. They attacked with fierce, committed violence. They attacked like combat engineers attacking trenchworks.

Lorenzo Secondari was the most feared and hated man in the entire Fiume regime. The rich were mauled by him, scarified, laid waste.

Of course the rich tried to save themselves from his persecutions. At first, they appeared at his new office, using any and every pretext. Then they eloquently begged him to stop his misdeeds.

When he blandly told the rich that they were welcome to work as laborers within their own factories, they gazed at him in utter horror. They despaired and ran away. Then they plotted reprisals.

When the persecuted wealthy of Fiume realized that Secondari could not be bribed, or corrupted, or persuaded, or reasoned with, they tried to kill him.

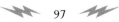

Copying his own methods (for they had quickly learned all about piracy), the Fiuman opposition bombed his staff car. Then they shot at him with pistols in a café. Finally, they tried to run him over with a cargo truck.

But Lorenzo Secondari proved unkillable. Since he had already been killed once, he knew that he was an Overman of Destiny. He went entirely unscathed. He was even happy to win the public reputation of a man who was bulletproof. The notoriety saved him a lot of work.

Frau Piffer, however, was enraged by the attacks on him. Always mild and timid for her own sake, Frau Piffer became a vengeful dragon when Secondari was imperilled.

Frau Piffer conceived the furious idea that Gigante, Grossich, Maylander, and Zanella—the grandees of Fiume—should all be arrested and publicly tried as Communists.

The wealthy elite of Fiume were certainly not Communists. But they were, in stark fact, a conspiratorial cell of anti-government subversives. So, once they were treated as Communists: jailed, ceaselessly interrogated, with all their papers seized, and denied any effective legal counsel; then Gigante, Grossich, Maylander, and Zanella simply crumbled in the dock.

At their extensive public show-trial, the wretched conspirators confessed to a weird variety of crimes: sabotage, attempted murder, Freemasonry, an intimate connection to Jewish bankers. Newsreel cameras whirred as the malefactors choked out their broken confessions. Radio microphones spread the drama by short-wave.

Secondari sat through the show-trial, occasionally testifying personally about the attempts on his life. He passed the time by reading back issues of *Popular Mechanics* and *Radio Experimenter.*

At length, the newly convicted criminals, in striped pyjamas with their heads shaven, were packed off in leg-irons to the desolate prison island of Isola Calva. This isle was a barren Adriatic slag-heap that the Carnaro regime successfully claimed, because nobody else wanted it.

VIII
THE REGENCY OF CARNARO, MAY 10, 1920– SEPTEMBER 6, 1920

HAVING OUTFOXED

ITS foreign adversaries and liquidated its internal opp- osition, the Regency of Carnaro had established itself as a modern, Twentieth- Century, European regime.

The Regency of Carnaro was a small but cruel nation, very much like the Balkan states that were its closest neighbors. Economically, the Regency was a free entrepôt. As a functional port, it worked about as well as most port cities within Italy did.

When it was stripped of its gorgeous symbols, its flags, flowers, and revolutionary rhetoric, its radio broadcasts and newsreels, its jackboot marches, its salutes, weird war cries and ceremonial mob scenes—seen very starkly, just as a realpolitik political machine—the Regency of Carnaro

was a clique of armed, dissolute poets who robbed bankers, then distributed the means of production to labor unions.

The leaders of Carnaro were hard, even brutal, authoritarians, who pretended to be flowery, musical, poetic anarchists.

Having arrived within the halls of power, Secondari realized all of this. He could never hear it very well, but he saw it perfectly. But he was not disillusioned or upset by what he saw. He was an engineer with power. Such was his powerful machine. His task was to make the machine run. It was a Syndicalist machine, because he owned it. Because he owned it, he was a Syndicalist.

Having seized the factories in town by force of arms, Secondari did his best to put the state industries on a practicable financial footing. Since he was a young engineer, and not a seasoned financier, he was quite bad at this. Instead of distributing utopian rewards to all and sundry, he had to cruelly repress dissent.

The Regency of Carnaro, as a small but nevertheless genuine nation, was no longer a revolutionary's dream. The labor unions running the factories (renamed as "Syndicates") were almost as incompetent as the capitalists had once been. Given genuine power over their own workplaces, the workers never worked very hard. They naturally preferred to grant themselves lavish health-care, free cafeterias, and long holidays.

The revolutionary Syndicalist factories—although some of the prettiest factories in the world—barely scraped along financially. Fiume was a modest, palmy river town adorning the sunny Adriatic. Fiume was entirely unsuited to become a natural center of heavy industry, such as Turin, Manchester, or Pittsburg. The Regency of Carnaro had to find other means of subsistence.

Since Carnaro was a regime of writers, much of the state's income naturally came from readers. The many readers of *Popolo d'Italia,* the Milanese political daily, had been especially generous to the Cause of Fiume.

Popolo d'Italia was therefore a propaganda organ of critical importance to the Regency of Carnaro. Sadly, the thriving newspaper had lost its founding editor, Benito Mussolini, in a domestic violence scandal. After much debate, though, a new editor was found: a younger man with a lighter and easier touch.

Mussolini's successor was "Yambo," or rather Enrico Novelli, the Genoese satirical cartoonist and film director.

Novelli's broad lampoons and his bright, upbeat editorials (commonly about marvels of science) caught the eye of a fresh Italian audience. Novelli tirelessly promoted the Regency of Carnaro as an offshore art colony and an exotic tourist destination.

Through this softer, kindlier approach, Fiume's tourist trade quickly boomed. First, Italians arrived, and then some French. Then came hordes of adventurous Americans, all laden with valuable dollars, flocking in to stare in awe at the strange bohemian goings-on.

Many of these Americans were Negro jazz musicians. The Negroes were startled to find themselves entirely welcome in Fiume as political refugees.

As international tensions eased, the American Navy ceased their nervous patrols of the Adriatic. The Italian Navy, suffering severe budget cuts, quickly followed.

Then the Italian government fell again. This common event surprised nobody. The snap elections produced results of utter political confusion in Italy. This too was rather predictable. The resulting technical caretaker government of Italy was headed by Senator Marconi.

The irascible, one-eyed radio genius was a poor administrator. However, Marconi was immensely popular in both Britain and America, so the English-speaking Great Powers gave Marconi a free hand in Italian affairs.

Guglielmo Marconi was a close personal friend of the Prophet—since one-eyed Italian geniuses had a natural commonality.

The Marconi parliament granted an amnesty to the Fiume military mutineers. Sensing the change in the wind, the homesick Italian troops began to depart from Fiume. First went the Alpini, welcomed home as heroes. Then the Sardinian grenadiers of the Seven of Ronchi marched off, their decision vindicated. General Valpini's military police were seen off by hordes of their weeping girlfriends.

Carnaro's finances quickly improved—for the host of Italian occupation soldiers had been a dead weight on the regime's budget. Only the "Desperates" remained in Fiume—as pirates turned police.

With the departure of Italian troops, globe-trotting foreign legionaries slunk into the town. These marauders crept in from every corner of the earth, for the news had spread that Carnaro could forge new passports. Carnaro loathed the very idea of world order. Extradition was unheard of.

So the refugee anarchists of the Bavarian Social Republic ventured to Carnaro. And the Hungarian Communists of Bela Kun came, too, and Gandhian mystics from the rebellious Congress of India. The Irish Republican Army were especially fond of Carnaro, now that their Easter Rebellion had become a bloody British civil war.

The people of Carnaro supported the Catalans, the Kurds, and the Flemish of Belgium. They sympathized with irredentist American Negroes in Harlem, especially those poetic souls who sought to return on Black Star ocean liners to Ethiopia.

As a minister of the government, Secondari liked to publicly attend the jazz clubs of Fiume. He went there often, black-clad, bearded, long-haired, and heavily armed. Secondari preferred jazz music to all other forms of music, because jazz was loud.

His sinister presence within the jazz clubs made it clear to all that American Negroes were under a particular protection in Fiume. The jazz clubs were also excellent places to discreetly meet international dealers in arms and narcotics.

Fiume was a wide-open, gun-running port for all the Croatian, Montenegrin, and Bosnian national guerrillas. The rebels against Yugoslavia swarmed in all the hills and isles of the Balkans. The Regency of Carnaro thrived, day by day, as the ramshackle fakery called "Yugoslavia" collapsed, night by night.

It was easy to see the poetic justice in the new world politics. The Serbs, through their own pirates, the "Black Hand" terrorist group, had started the holocaust of the Great War. The Great War of the Titans—reduced at last to its original struggle, among the Balkan pygmies—would end, finally, on Serbia's own bloodstained soil.

The Great War would end, at last, within Serbia, and not in the Paris Peace Talks. The Great War could only end where the Great War had begun: if, indeed, any war in Europe could ever be said to truly end at all.

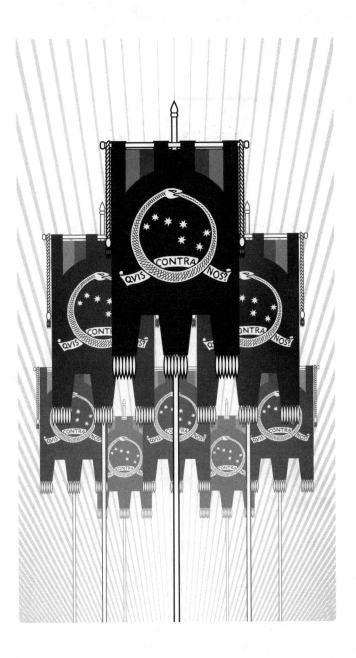

4: THE PLATONIC LOVERS

IX
THE REGENCY OF CARNARO,
SEPTEMBER 9, 1920

DESPITE THE GREAT
change in their personal
circumstances, Secondari still
valued the friendship of Frau Piffer.
Frau Piffer's homespun wisdom, her intimate knowledge of Fiuman customs and
habits, was of great use to Secondari. She had
often spared him the annoying trouble of shooting people.

Secondari knew that he was feared and hated.
After all, this was obviously the basic purpose of a
"Minister of Vengeance Weapons." Frau Piffer, by
contrast to everyone else, did not fear him. She was
infallibly kind to him. She had looked after him, even
nursed him and fed him when he had been at his weakest
and his worst. This was more than his own family had ever
done for him.

Times had changed. Lorenzo Secondari was no longer a weak, hungry, and wounded ex-soldier. Thanks to the hospitality, the decent food, the balmy weather, and the healing salt air of Fiume, he was healthy and strong.

Although he would never hear well again, he was a powerful, war-hardened, even ferocious, armed revolutionary. So people were right to fear him. Frau Piffer, though, was also a successful revolutionary. Frau Piffer was the only woman he knew who could talk simply and frankly to him about work.

Though he sometimes thought of going back to Turin— he had left important things undone, back in Italy—he could not abandon the many fine things that he and Frau Piffer had achieved together.

Understanding this situation, Secondari resolved to renounce his Italian citizenship. He arranged to meet Frau Piffer in her dazzling new office at the Flying Radio Torpedo Factory. He told her that he, too, wanted to become a citizen of the Regency of Carnaro, like herself. He told her that he, too, wanted to become a model of Futurism, as it was properly lived.

He asked her to arrange the paperwork, for she excelled at such things, and she agreed. He and Frau Piffer would become two ideal Carnarians. When all was said and done, he was an engineer, while she was a manufacturer. A man and woman occupying those two roles had a proper need for an intimate understanding.

X
THE REGENCY OF CARNARO,
SEPTEMBER 11, 1920

THE ACE OF HEARTS

sent Secondari a confi-
dential memo by the inter-office
mail. This covert message alerted
Secondari to the long-expected arrival
of the American Secret Service.

It had taken the Americans eight long months
to overcome their grave diplomatic embarrassment,
and approach the Carnaro regime. The Americans
were new to the burdens of a Great Power, but they
were trying. An American spy group was arriving within
deep cover, to quietly discuss American national interests.

The leader of this American spy delegation was a superhuman Jew. This fantastic figure was known worldwide as
the "Man Without Fear."

The Man Without Fear was a black magician. Although
he was clearly a supernatural entity, he was also a naturalized

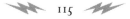

American citizen. The magician spy was bringing two spy associates: they posed as his bodyguard and his public-relations expert.

The American spy-magician was arriving in the city of Fiume—not secretly at all—but in the distracting glare of a giant blaze of publicity. The magical entertainment of the Man Without Fear would be held within the biggest venue in Fiume. This was the Prophet's own palatial City Hall, which had been placed entirely at the spy's disposal.

The Man Without Fear was the greatest magician in the modern world. He was a conjurer on a vast, American, continental scale. Magicians said that the Man Without Fear was the greatest magician in the history of magic.

Unfortunately, the American magician spoke no Italian. So Secondari, who spoke and wrote English well, was much-needed to assist with the intrigue.

Although Secondari was deaf, his handicap had slowly diminished with time. His right ear had grown sensitive to bass vibration, and he'd learned to patch together every scrap of sound from his good left ear. Frau Piffer's patient help in this regard had been of great use to him. He'd even learned homely scraps of Croatian and German from little Maria Piffer.

To confront the American spies, Secondari would need the sturdy aid of Frau Piffer. He knew that he could trust her. So he sent her a telegram, requesting her presence at his secret police office in the Hotel Europa.

To his surprise, for the first time ever, Frau Piffer did not answer him.

Alarmed, he sought Frau Piffer at her mother's house. Frau Piffer's mother, whose full name he had never learned, was a weird Fiuman crone. This ancient Adriatic creature, still in her time-worn native costume of apron, shawl, and crimped head-cloth, had long gray wisps of hair, no remaining teeth, and fishy, flounder-like eyes set a full hands-width apart. Frau Piffer's mother looked quite like Frau Piffer, though in a state of advanced decay.

This crone often served as Maria's babysitter while her mother was busy manufacturing. The three of them, the grandmother, mother, and daughter, occupied a homey medieval nook within the Fiume Old Town. They lived within a damp, stony cell about the size of a Turinese automobile garage.

Secondari arrived at the medieval slum in his violently glittering Futurist uniform. Secondari's attempt to dress for diplomacy with the Americans had been, at best, a mixed success. He hated his elaborate, garish new uniform, and his new haircut disgusted him. The frightened barber had hidden Secondari's damaged right ear by giving him a long forelock, which swooped across his forehead. Worse yet, his unkempt, bristling, piratical beard had been reduced to a neat, oddly tiny mustache.

Secondari knocked, entered, and found Frau Piffer as a shattered wreckage of nerves. She was beside herself with misery.

Secondari sat at her narrow bedside as Frau Piffer choked out her tale of woe.

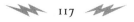

Frau Piffer's erring husband had come to grief. Herr Piffer, a career Communist agitator, had fled from Fiume to Red Vienna. In Vienna, he'd made the streets too hot for himself. Fool that he was, he'd run off straight to Berlin. In Berlin, the radical street-brawls were deadly.

"Oh, this must be all my own fault," Frau Piffer wailed. "Herr Piffer seemed so noble and good, and I let him have his way with me. So then we had Maria, and off he ran to smash the state, the wretch! Not one day's honest work out of him at the factory line, and now he's in jail! Whatever will I do?"

"Well, first, calm down, my dear," Secondari counselled, patting her plump hand. "He's in jail again, is he? That means he's not dead. So there must be hope."

Frau Piffer proffered a tear-soaked letter. The letter was useless to Secondari, being written entirely in German. "He threw in his lot with some crowd of German ex-soldiers. Those Freikorps people, they're real street thugs. My Hans is just a factory worker! Oh my God, he's my husband, my child's father! I loved him so, Lorenzo! I lived for those few sweet days when Hans came back to me! Now I'm abandoned! I'm even worse than a widow."

Maria was also weeping bitterly, stunned by her mother's distress. The withered grandmother, seeing Frau Piffer grasping Secondari's hand and sobbing pitifully on his uniform sleeve, tactfully rose. She tottered from the meager apartment.

"I know that you're upset just now," said Secondari, "but let's take counsel together. Be strong, Blanka Piffer. Think of the child here. Herr Piffer's in prison, is he? He's facing a trial? What are the charges? Be specific."

"It's the worst," said Frau Piffer, sitting up and plumping her embroidered pillow. "Some German faction in a beer cellar... Their own men, the 'Brown Shirts'... They burst in there with guns and big knives, a massacre! His best friend—Adolf from Linz, such a brave soldier—he jumped in front of a bullet, to save my husband. Adolf gave his own life for my Hans."

The thought made Frau Piffer weep piteously. "I met Adolf once. He came here on a summer vacation with Hans. He was the best of them all, Adolf was. What a talker that man was, and what eyes he had!"

"The Austrians should never have anything to do with Germans, ever," Secondari said. "Whenever you mess with the Germans, you always end up in debt to them, shining their shoes."

"Well, Adolf was from Linz. Adolf was Austrian, himself."

"Let's get to the point now," said Secondari. "Frau Piffer, we are both professional revolutionaries. We're not children, so let Maria do the crying. We are in power, and your husband is in prison. Fine. Now, we act."

Secondari raised one gloved finger, white kid gloves being de rigueur for evening wear at Regency of Carnaro social events. "Listen. We raise funds, Frau Piffer. We set up solidarity committees. We agitate in the world press. As government officials, we can put on diplomatic pressure. We will embarrass the German government in Berlin—until they realize it's not worth their while to hold Herr Piffer. They will exile him here: they'll send him here, to us, to the Regency of Carnaro. This town is full of political exiles. One more exile, your husband, will be just fine here!"

Frau Piffer wiped at her eyes with her quilt. "You really think we can do that?"

"Of course! Look at yourself, woman! You're a Corporate Syndicalist! And I'm a government minister; look at my fancy uniform! I chase my regime's enemies into exile every day! We both know how that's done. Of course we can do it. We can, and we will. Have faith in tomorrow."

Frau Piffer, gathering her strength, looked at her German letter again. "Maybe we really can do that. My husband's friend, who wrote me this nice letter from the jail... He's so eloquent! He's a novelist, you see. Herr Goebbels."

"Good, fine, now you're talking some sense. This German political novelist, no doubt he's in hot water, too. So, bring him down here to Fiume. We'll find this political correspondent a post somewhere. Let's put him to work. We can always use more spies inside Germany."

Frau Piffer's lips were trembling. "You are such a good man, Lorenzo. I was so lucky to meet you. I'm an atheist and a Communist, but you are the answer to a woman's prayers. Saint Vitus of Fiume must love me after all."

Secondari smiled, then shrugged. "Everything I'm telling you now is simple and obvious. If you weren't so upset, you would know that better than I do."

"No, that's not true. You are such a marvel. I was lying here in my blackest despair, you are my angel, Lorenzo...

I don't know how to tell you this, but really, truly, you are my hero."

She kissed his hand. Maria rose to her feet and hugged his waist.

He patted the child's braided blonde head. Maria had quickly stopped her sobs and sniffles. Although Maria would never be a great beauty, she was a sturdy, workaday, patchwork-and-polyglot little creature. He doted on Maria. She was the light of his life.

"Lorenzo, isn't there something I can do to reward you?" Frau Piffer moaned. "I know that I'm a married woman, while you are so chaste and honorable. But I would do anything for you, my knight, my man of destiny! There is a statue of you in my heart!"

This abject fit of eloquence was the most Italian moment he had ever seen from Frau Piffer. Secondari was touched.

"Well," he said at last, "there is something that I have never told you about, Frau Piffer. I don't know how to say it in front of this innocent child, though."

"So, is there something?" said Frau Piffer, blinking. "I knew there must be something! Maria, run out and go play."

The child obediently left her mother, although she was scowling. Secondari glimpsed her tear-streaked little pirate face, spying through the wooden shutters of the stone window.

"This was an entirely private matter," he told her. "It happened in Turin, years ago. I've never gotten over the shame."

"I always knew that there must be something wrong about you. I'm a Fiume girl, all right? We live by the docks!

We Fiume girls don't shock easily. Just tell me what it is."

"My whole family should be ashamed of what happened. I'm ashamed that they don't have more shame! Turin is full of dark and awful secrets. That's the kind of town it is, not like this one."

"Don't make me guess!" Frau Piffer cried. "Whatever awful sin it is, just tell me now."

"My brother in Turin has a bastard child. He seduced a factory girl. Then he abandoned her."

Secondari gritted his teeth. "Everyone in Turin adores my brother. Because he's rich, he's influential, and he's in high society. He is the Great and the Good—and yet, he's the picture of evil, that man. My brother got away with his crime. He escaped all retribution. No one cares. And in Turin, there's a little boy—he's younger than Maria, even—and he's of my own blood. He's the child of a bitter injustice."

"Oh, well, I see," said Frau Piffer. "Well, that's quite a common story. I thought you would tell me something awful."

"I never breathed one word of this scandal to anybody. How can any man be so wicked? He's my own brother! I hope you can see that I'm entirely decent, unlike him. I would never do such a thing. I would die first."

"Lorenzo, I understand. What is it you want me to do?"

"Well, maybe we can go to Turin, you and I. We can bring back that boy, to live here, in Fiume. We might bring his mother, too, if she wants to come here. I know I can't raise a son. I don't know how to do it. But you can raise children. You're kind and good. Maria is a wonderful child.

We'll adopt that little boy. We'll pirate him. We'll syndicate him. He'll become ours."

"But we're not married, Lorenzo. How can we adopt a boy? We can't just march into the city of Turin with our strange uniforms, and say we're from the Regency of Carnaro, and we're here to take the future away with us."

"Oh yes, we can. We must do exactly that. Because we have to live by our convictions, Frau Piffer! You, and me, and Maria, and my bastard nephew. We will never be any bourgeois, legal family. But we can become a free syndicate of liberated people who unite in defiance of the Church and the State!"

Secondari drew a deep breath. "Some day, in the Twentieth Century ahead of us, most families—maybe all the families!—will be like us. I want you at my side as we lead the way to that better way of life!"

"Well, of course I must say 'yes' to you," said Frau Piffer. "So, yes, of course I will do it. Another strange boy in my life, some boy who is just like you...well, I will bear up somehow! But Lorenzo, please leave me alone now. That noble speech you just gave me—it was too much! My heart is bursting! You're like the Prophet, almost."

"Oh, come now. I'm an engineer. I am nothing like the Prophet."

"No, really, you are very like a great poet. Maybe something about the Prophet has touched you, and changed you forever, and now... Well, my poor heart is in my mouth. My head is spinning. I'm so torn by my feelings now, I don't know what to say."

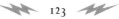

"Let's try to be content, Frau Piffer. You've made me very happy through your act of social justice."

Three steps were enough to take him from the shabby stone cell. He opened the door, and saw Maria lurking out in the cobbled alley.

He reached down to grip her hand. "Come along now, Maria. Come along with me tonight, we're going to see magic!"

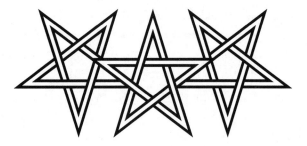

5: THE MAN WITHOUT FEAR

XI
THE REGENCY OF CARNARO,
SEPTEMBER 11, 1920

THE CITY HALL,

a veritable palace of ur-
ban administration, had always
been much too large for the city of
Fiume. The City Hall had been built to
a regal, theatrical scale, as if little Fiume
ranked with Venice, the Queen of the Adriatic.

The City Hall had marble staircases, and
carved balustrades, and life-sized, half-naked bronze
lantern-girls brandishing lit candelabra. It had par-
quet flooring, and ceilings with huge, writhing octopus
chandeliers of blown Murano glass.

Secondari took the astonished Maria by her small hand.
He pretended to give her a tour of the palace. In reality, he
was searching the City Hall for the Prophet and his inner
circle. Secondari needed to offer his services in the secret
meeting with the American spies.

Secondari knew that he was badly needed for that diplomatic effort, but the crowds in City Hall were so thick that he couldn't find anyone. It seemed that everyone in Fiume had crowded in to see the great American magician.

Secondari entered the capacious chamber where the American magician was shortly to perform. A special magical stage had been built there, designed to the American's express commands, sent in by telegram.

This naked wooden stage was saturated with magical American contraptions. Strange, elaborate machines designed to vanish volunteers, or perhaps to saw the women of Fiume into quarreling halves.

The seats of the audience radiated from this stage of American gadgetry, with palatial chairs arranged in front, and modest benches set in the back. Workers in angular Futurist uniforms were hauling electrical cables. Others laid out red carpets, and tried the curtain-pulleys.

A ghastly apparition peered from behind a velvet curtain of the stage. She beckoned urgently at Secondari. Secondari instantly recognized her as one of the Prophet's harem of mistresses. This woman was the Art Witch.

The Art Witch was a Milanese millionairess and ardent occultist. She was a fixture in the European radical art world. The Art Witch was so entirely weird and eldritch that even the Ace of Hearts, a fellow Milanese who was a yogi, a nudist, a vegetarian, and a pirate, could not bear the sight of her.

The Art Witch beckoned again, frantically, and Secondari, wisely averting his gaze, pretended a profound deafness.

The Art Witch, however, was a spoilt and determined woman, ever eager to have her own way. She came teetering from the stage, in her dagger-like high heels, to compel his attention.

The Art Witch was wearing—not a dress, but a strange, provocative curtain of some kind, made from dense strings of shining metal beads. This bizarre garment lacked any visible bustle, or a girdle, or a brassiere, or, quite likely, underwear of any kind.

The Art Witch was very thin and tall, with high-piled, dyed red hair in tumbling snaky locks. Her dilated black eyes were entirely surrounded by huge circles of black kohl. Her skin was powdered whiter than a corpse. Her rings and bracelets had enough jewels to buy an Italian battleship.

The Art Witch stared down at little Maria, who was thunderstruck by the apparition before her. Maria clung tightly to Secondari's right elbow. Then, in a paroxysm of terrified shyness, she hung from his arm and pivoted back and forth.

"You have a new haircut, Pirate Engineer," said the Art Witch.

"You look as radiant as always, Marchesa." Secondari never knew what to say to the Prophet's doxies. So, he flattered them. The approach always seemed to work.

"Where is the Prophet tonight?" said the Art Witch.

"Did you ask your crystal ball?" said Secondari. "If you can't find him with your magic powers, no one can."

The Art Witch turned and beckoned sharply. A second woman arrived from her nook behind the velvet stage-curtain.

This fellow-creature of the art-world was costumed as a Moslem dancing girl, with trailing, diaphanous silk robes, a veil, a hood, and a pearl-inlaid leather holster with a dainty pistol inside.

"What a pretty daughter your friend has here, Luisa," said the Art Witch's armed companion. "Do you like dancing, little girl?"

"Yes, signora," Maria lisped, turning up her face from Secondari's uniform sleeve.

"That's good," said the veiled concubine, writhing expertly, "because I am the Dancer of the Future."

Secondari cast a swift glance at the dancer's pistol. "You are Valentine de Saint-Point," he said. "My agents told me that you were in Cairo."

"Now you've gone and spoilt my surprise," said the Art Witch. "Valentine came here to Fiume, just to help me liberate the World Anima from her bondage."

Secondari said nothing. It was entirely characteristic of the Art Witch to show up in Fiume with a wanted fugitive. It was very like the kind-hearted Prophet to forgive, and shelter, such a woman. The Regency of Carnaro had no extradition agreements.

"You used to be much nicer to me, Pirate Engineer," the Art Witch pouted. "Such a well-brought-up, middle-class Turinese boy."

Secondari quietly absorbed this insult. He wasn't entirely sure what the Art Witch had said to him. Possibly, he had imagined the insult. "Well, the Future changes people, Marchesa."

"Have you heard about 'Dada' yet?" the Art Witch prodded.

"I'm just an engineer."

He didn't have to wait long for the Art Witch to enlighten him about Dada. "They're great artists from Paris and Zurich. Much more up-to-date than our former friend—that self-styled avant-gardiste—that pompous has-been, Signor Marinetti."

"Signor Marinetti is a brave Italian soldier. Are they soldiers, these Dada friends of yours?"

"Oh yes, Lieutenant," said the Art Witch. "They're all ex-soldiers, every last one of them. And their leader is a soldier's psychiatrist!"

"To fire a gun at random into a crowd," said the Dancer of the Future, "is the ultimate artistic act of Dada."

"I don't want to keep you two ladies from your night out on the town," said Secondari. He had achieved a miracle of tact with this statement, but both the women entirely ignored him. They were gazing raptly over his shoulder.

Being deaf, Secondari hadn't heard the approaching footsteps. The sudden presence at his elbow was yet another stunningly beautiful woman. She was the movie actress, Pina Menichelli.

Even the Dancer of the Future was impressed by the radiantly glamorous appearance of the movie star. The Art Witch blinked her colossal black eyes, and simpered at the diva. "So, how are you, Giuseppina?"

"I'm looking for that American magician," said the movie star. "I want to pay him a courtesy call. Because he makes movies, like I do."

"We're looking for the Prophet, instead," said the Art Witch. "Have you seen the Prophet?"

"Of course I have," said La Menichelli. "I came here from Turin, along with His Highness the Duke. The Prophet met our royal entourage at the railway station. He was very kind to us."

"I'm from Turin," Secondari offered numbly. He was astounded by the actress's unearthly beauty.

Still, Pina Menichelli was somewhat shorter than he would have guessed. The actress also seemed to have put on some weight.

"What a sweet little girl," said the movie star. Pina Menichelli had a broad Neapolitan accent, which was never apparent in her many silent films. "So, is that your peasant costume, little girl? I swear, the way you people dress here in Fiume, it beats anything on my shooting sets."

The Art Witch interrupted. "My friend here—he's the Minister of Vengeance Weapons—he was just about to give us some of the needful," she said. "I'm sure you have some fairy dust to share with us, Signor Minister."

Reluctantly, trapped by the circumstances, Secondari handed over a glass vial of cocaine.

"Only two grams?" said the Art Witch.

"Cocaine is a Vengeance Weapon," Secondari explained. "So we need to restrict this valuable substance to those who have high-speed driving skills and weapons training."

"I can drive very fast indeed," said the Dancer of the Future, patting her pistol.

"Oh, I don't need any of that stuff," said the movie star.

"Oh, wait, fine. I'll take a little for my husband. The Baron has to work tomorrow. He's scouting out locations here in Fiume, poor dear."

"Congratulations on your marriage," said the Art Witch. "How many husbands does this make for you, Pina?"

The Dancer of the Future burst into melodious giggles. "Oh Luisa, stop being so clever! You're really so bad!"

"Are you married any more, Valentine?"

"Me? Never! I'm a Futurist Moslem concubine! I'd rather be skinned than get married! Especially to some Italian."

The Art Witch deftly popped open the cocaine vial. Then, using a tiny gold spoon from her bodice, she ladled a generous helping into a dry cigarette paper. She deftly sealed it, with a long, serpentine lick.

She handed the paper-wrapped cocaine bundle to the actress. "Pina, my pretty dancer friend here is also a famous writer." The Art Witch blinked her enormous eyes at the movie star. "I strongly advise you to read her *Manifesto of Futurist Lust*. To your husband. In bed, of course. As an occult prophetess, I can assure you, that will work wonders."

The movie star took the drugs, silently turned on her high heel, and stalked away.

"My God, what a pill she's become now. That washed-up Lady of Spasms, that former femme fatale," said the Dancer of the Future to the Art Witch. "Did you see how much weight she's put on? She'll never get before the camera in her condition."

The Art Witch touched her powdered forehead with one lacquered fingertip. "I can sense, yes, I foresee, that Pina

Menichelli will leave the world of cinema entirely. Did you see all those nasty little lines around her eyes? She's been at it long enough."

"Luisa, do you want to stay here to see Houdini?" said the Dancer.

"No, no, I already saw Houdini in Rome," scoffed the Art Witch. "Not one shred of true occultism in Houdini's whole act! It's all cheap American gadget tricks! He's a fraud! He does tricks fit for children!"

"Then let's go to that jazz club, down by the docks," said the Dancer eagerly. "Anita Berber is performing tonight."

"Should I know that woman?"

"Anita Berber? She's only the greatest nude dancer in the whole world! Anita is a complete degenerate! She's fresh from Berlin."

"That sounds quite tasteful," said the Art Witch. "I bet this overwrought soldier-boy would love to come along with us to see that."

"This is my daughter," said Secondari. "She wants to see the magic tricks fit for children."

"Why are you Turinese always like this? You're even worse than the Swiss!" said the Art Witch. "If you didn't have so many séances in Turin, with all your genuine dark, dead spirits, I would never forgive you people. Never mind. You come along now, Valentine."

They left.

XII
THE REGENCY OF CARNARO,
SEPTEMBER 11, 1920

SECONDARI FOUND

FRONT-ROW seats at the
magic show for both himself and
his daughter. There was some trouble
about that with the ushers, but Secondari
was not the most feared man in Fiume for
nothing.

The great hall was packed to capacity. Many
eager people were turned away. The Prophet's black-
clad Desperate bodyguards had to chase them off in
groups and clusters. Then—for the Prophet was always
indulgent to them—the Desperates were allowed to sit
on the floor.

Then the regime arrived in the hall, in a great, glittering line. Secondari immediately realized that, as the most
hated man in Fiume, he had been left out of this crucial
political arrangement.

They marched in from backstage: the Prophet himself, the Ace of Hearts, the Constitutionalist, the Foreign Minister, and the Jewish Economist. Then a round dozen of the other, less-legendary, regime figures.

All of these men were dressed with exceeding dignity. They stood before their velvet chairs, and they all remained standing, looking stiff and anxious.

A sudden fanfare rang out. Like everyone else in the hall, Secondari leapt at once to his feet. He dragged his daughter upright. "Royalty!" he told her.

The Duke of Aosta strode into the hall, in full military uniform, with a shining sash, heroic medals, and thick braids of gold at the shoulders.

The Duke of Aosta was the cousin of the King of Italy. During the Great War, the Duke had been the fiercely ardent commander of the Italian Third Army.

The Third Army—it was Secondari's own army—was the Italian army that had fought the hardest, and bled the most. The Duke of Aosta was a true Savoy warrior. He was a martial aristocrat who killed his nation's enemies in droves. The Duke of Aosta was much more stern and bellicose than his milder cousin, the King.

The Duke was also younger, taller, and more handsome than the reigning King of Italy. Unlike the King, who never risked his royal dignity, the dashing Duke of Aosta flew combat aircraft with his own hands.

The Duke of Aosta was skilled at every branch of modern arms. Through the Duke's royal favor, the Prophet had also shared in that warlike dignity. The Prophet had served in the Italian Army, and the Italian Flying Corps, and in the Italian Navy, as well. It was thanks to the Duke of Aosta that the Prophet had managed all these unorthodox military reassignments.

The royal Duke saw fit to seat himself among his uniformed Futurist hosts. Then the large civilian crowd also sat, murmuring in awe and wonderment.

Nothing had been said aloud. No arrangement had been formally announced. But the gesture was entirely legible.

The "Regency of Carnaro" was about to become a genuine Regency. There could be no other explanation for the Duke's presence within the hall. The pirate utopia of Fiume was taking shelter under the millennium-long prestige of the Savoy Dynasty. The Future was safely in the gloved hands of the oldest royal line in the world.

The Prophet, showing an unusual modesty, tactfully sat three seats distant from Carnaro's future Prince-Regent. Supported by the stays beneath his tailored uniform, the great poet sat up ramrod-straight.

Gazing at the great visionary, Secondari suddenly realized, to his own surprise, that he could read the poet's soul. Although he was just an engineer, his deafness had, somehow, taught him that knack.

He could read the Prophet's aged face like an open book. The Prophet was miserable.

The Prophet wore his tinted glasses, as he often did for daylight, as these stage-lights hurt his single good eye. The Prophet tugged at the cuffs of his flawless gloves. He fondled his leather swagger stick. These agitated gestures revealed

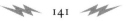

the truth to Secondari. The Prophet's soul was black, and curdled, and biting itself in a mystical torment.

The Prophet was disgusted. He was an Overman, and yet he was bored. Being an Overman, he had a vast, decadent, hapless, all-consuming, spiritual boredom. Although the triumph he had prophesied was coming to pass—a magnificent victory won, in the teeth of the entire League of Nations—the Prophet was unsatisfied. To prophesy was not to enjoy.

Now that he had won his victory, the Prophet looked as hollow as a rotten tree. He was no ruler. The Duke of Aosta was the ruler. In the shadow of a competent ruler, a Prophet was merely a poet. The Prophet was superhuman, and yet he was doomed.

The Prophet would end up even worse than Garibaldi had ended. He would be blind, weak, sick, surrounded by his decadent clutter, the plaything of his own female playthings. An almighty creature, but without any dignity. A much-respected hero, devoid of any self-respect.

The stage lights went up. The stage band struck up a fanfare. The Man Without Fear took command of the stage.

The great American illusionist was dressed in a white tie and tails. He was short, muscular, and entirely vigorous. He looked quite Jewish.

The magician addressed the hushed crowd, speaking Italian. This was a passable, phonetic recitation that he had clearly memorized for the occasion. He then uttered some brief remarks in Austrian German, a language he knew well, being Austrian by birth.

Entirely at ease on his self-designed magic stage, the Man Without Fear began his magic act with a few standard card tricks.

Little Maria Piffer was entertained to the last degree by this. She squirmed with childish joy on the edge of her velvet chair. She wildly applauded along with the audience. Maria had never had such a good time.

Secondari gazed on her fondly. He took comfort in her innocent pleasure, her lack of adult cynicism, her rapture at the American's grotesque illusions. He had done something for Maria that she would never forget in her life. This bonded them even more, somehow.

He was proud to be sitting with Maria, instead of sitting in that row of stiffs, with the regime. He and Maria were in the presence of royalty together. His little pirate, Maria, had not so much as washed her face or combed her tangled hair. In her little pinafore—it was threadbare, though dutifully patched by her mama—she was like a dandelion in the sidewalk.

He glanced from her eager face to the somber ranks of the functionaries of the Regency of Carnaro. Imprisoned within their fine uniforms, and by the dignity of their own event, all of them—even the leonine Ace of Hearts—looked like Sicilian stage-puppets.

They had become a government. And yet no government—especially an Italian one—was ever really loved and obeyed. Every Italian government was nine-tenths charade.

He, too, was a part of that government, but since he was still an unrepentant pirate, he was the most hated one. They

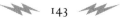

all hated and feared him, to some greater or lesser degree. Except for Maria Piffer.

No one in Fiume loved Secondari without any question. Nobody did whatever he said to do, with all the unthinking and total respect that was due to an Overman. But Maria did that.

For Maria Piffer, he was truly a mysterious, all-powerful hero. He had come from nowhere into her childish life of deprivation. He was possessed of a knowledge far beyond her grasp.

He loved Maria.

This effusion of love within him did not make him a better man. On the contrary, his love made him realize that he would cheerfully kill anybody—even the entire Fiume regime, in their stuffed suits—for the sake of the child he loved.

He was no mere pirate of expedience, some gangster doing the will of other, better men. He was an entirely genuine, heartfelt, and totalitarian pirate. He hated every form of property. He loved every kind of theft.

He was the only member of the pirate government who was not some recuperated loyalist, seeking the world's respect. He was the genuine menace among them. He could burn, and crush, and blast, and smash anything, anywhere, without warning and without restraint. He was a human bomb.

With a practiced gesture, the Man Without Fear flung his magic deck of cards into the air. These cards—jacks, queens, kings, they were obviously real, royal cards—hung there, well above the magician's head. They wobbled a little, in the midst of the air, like aerial snowflakes.

The Man Without Fear walked around the cards, three times. He urged the cards to obey the law of gravity, and fall on him. The cards obeyed no law. They simply hung up there. Regally.

The Man Without Fear had to call for his stage assistant. This youngster was not the standard pretty girl within a magical entourage. He was a burly American teen. The American lad was dressed as a stage cowboy, complete with hat and boots.

The young cowboy brought the magician a chair and a bullwhip. The Man Without Fear brandished the chair, then cracked the whip. The magically suspended cards transformed into paper flowers. They flew upward, out of sight.

The crowd gasped. Maria was agape with amazement. Even the stiffly formal legionnaires of Carnaro lost their composure.

The Man Without Fear had done the impossible. He had performed an act that lacked any rational explanation.

The Man Without Fear paused in his magic routine. Speaking a halting Italian, he made a few complimentary remarks about the Pope. He had just met the Pope, apparently, while performing in Rome.

His Grace the Duke of Aosta saw fit to applaud the pious remarks. Others followed the Duke's lead.

The Man Without Fear then commenced to do quite impossible things with the chair—standing on it, balancing,

passing his hands through it. He deftly combined the chair, and the whip, in various practiced ways.

Secondari watched the illusions with all the close care that he could muster.

He saw no trace of any possible trickery. No wires, no mirrors, and no smoke. Cordially, the great magician went out of his way to prove the plangent wooden soundness of the chair. His amazing whip was merely a humble thing of leather.

The cowboy assistant arrived again, during stormy applause. He gave the magician an everyday sewing kit. The boy removed the chair and the whip from the stage.

The magician opened the sewing kit. He did a number of incredible things with the simple black and white spools of thread.

He then removed four pincushions from within his wicker basket. Every one of these dainty cushions bristling with many sharp steel needles. The magician paused to devour a set of steel pins, a stunt which amused Maria enormously.

The magician had the house lights turned up to full glare. He stepped right to the edge of his stage.

The Man Without Fear then proceeded to thrust the sharp steel needles straight into his own human face. Entirely calm and composed—he even spoke a little Italian as he did this awful feat—he jabbed the needles through his cheeks, through his eyebrows, through both his ears, and through the loose skin of his clean-shaven jowls.

He even thrust a large and particularly cruel steel needle entirely through his own nose. The needle went through one nostril, through the septum, and out the other side, the second nostril visibly bulging as the sharp needle-point stretched it and popped through.

The magician then left the magic stage. Deliberately, humbly, simply, he wandered before the front ranks of his audience. An American Jew with a face full of needles. He bristled like a hedgehog.

Slowly—after viewer after viewer had stared at him in fascinated repulsion—the magician came to stand directly before Secondari.

Noting Secondari's hostile and skeptical stare, the magician smiled urbanely. His steel-pierced cheeks twitched horribly. Then he bowed. He offered Secondari a fresh needle, and turned his cheek.

Maria shrieked in high-pitched, childish terror. The child wilted like a rag-doll, fainting where she sat. She toppled from her velvet chair. Secondari caught her as she tumbled.

Secondari rose with the child within his arms. Sympathetic cries burst from the ladies in the audience. Women fanned themselves in distress at the enormity. Several women swooned.

Alert to the mishap, the magician's cowboy assistant bounded down from the stage. Efficiently, he urged Secondari—with this fainting child still draped in his arms—up the stairs and to the stage.

The cowboy led them slowly across the stage, in full view of the audience. Then, finally, he led them behind the draped curtains.

"I can carry her now, sir," the cowboy offered, in English.

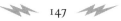

"I am her father," Secondari replied, in the same language.

"So, can you speak American? That's great! We'll take the little lady over to the dressing room. These things happen sometimes. I've seen this before, sir."

Out on his bright-lit stage, the Man Without Fear, entirely unperturbed and even urbane, was plucking the steel needles from his punctured face, then publicly eating them.

"Your maestro," said Secondari, easing into his rusty English, "is the greatest magician that I see, ever. What kind of man is that man?"

"Well, he's the greatest wizard in our modern world," said the cowboy with pride. "Because he's a Twentieth-Century wizard. His feats are all done with Knowledge and Science."

"His face," said Secondari. "My little girl...so much fear...."

"Oh, well, those needles aren't black magic," chuckled the cowboy. "Houdini just toughs that out!" The boy assistant made a sturdy bicep under his checked cowboy shirt. "See, it's all about physical training! Because he's a superman!"

The cowboy led them through the rear door of the hall, then down a short corridor.

6: THE GLORIOUS UTOPIA

XIII
THE REGENCY OF CARNARO,
SEPTEMBER 11, 1920

SECONDARI RECOGNIZED THE magician's dressing room. It was one of the Prophet's own private offices. This office had a scrolled leather davenport for the Prophet's frequent naps. It also had a polished teak desk and a posh white telephone.

The brocaded walls held a large collection of lethal Arditi daggers, and a startling number of blue faience Chinese jars.

Inside this borrowed office, another of the magician's assistants was busily typing away, using two fingers, in reporter-style. The typist glanced up from his code-book.

"Oh my word," he said alertly. He hopped up and cleared a suitcase from the davenport. Then he helped Secondari to set Maria onto the fine leather. The Prophet's couch was butter-soft, wrinkled, and covered with fine silk buttons.

"So, the old needle trick, was it?" said the reporter to the cowboy.

"Yup. You betcha."

"Does this guy in this weird, eldritch uniform speak any English?" said the reporter.

"A little, I reckon," said the cowboy.

"I understand you," said Secondari, putting his hand to his good ear. "But please, speak good, and also speak loud."

The typist looked Secondari up and down, squinting alertly. "Say, I think I've been briefed about you, sir! Aren't you Colonel Secondari, the weapons minister?"

"Yes," said Secondari. He was not a colonel, but that was a minor matter.

"Then I am very pleased to meet you, sir! I am Howard Lovecraft, Mr. Houdini's publicity agent. This young galoot is Mr. Robert Ervin Howard, from Cross Plains, Texas."

"Benvenuti a Fiume," Secondari muttered. He bent to look after Maria.

The poor child had soiled herself while unconscious. Secondari, who knew the City Hall well, left and found the nearest washroom. He returned with towels. He saw to the child's comfort and decency. Then he covered her with his military jacket.

"You know what, Bob?" said Lovecraft to Howard. "Those jaspers at the State Department have tried to make monkeys out of us! This is General Secondari here. He's supposed to be the most feared man in the whole regime. But he's a fine young father, with a little girl. Look at him! I'm touched by this."

"She looks so still, just lying there," said young Howard mournfully. "She reminds me a lot of my mom."

"The show's almost over. The boss is not gonna top that needle bit tonight," said Howard briskly. "So, you run on out to the street there, Bob. Fetch the little lady one of those vanilla ice-creams. That'll bring her around."

"Yes sir, Mr. Lovecraft," said the cowboy. He departed at a trot.

"He's a nice kid, Two-Gun Bob, but he's always going on about his mom," Lovecraft explained. "I've got a kid myself, you know. Just like you do, Colonel. Mrs. Lovecraft, she saw fit to present me with a fine young boy. Young Master Lovecraft has completely changed my life."

"Childs are the future," said Secondari in English. Maria Piffer began to stir. Secondari sat on the soft leather couch. He chafed her wrists, then patted her forehead. He murmured reassurances.

"Children are the future, that's entirely correct. It's thanks to little Ricky Lovecraft that I went into the advertising business. I sell progress, and my business is good."

Secondari fixed the spy with a level stare. "Your maestro is a secret agent of the United States of America."

Lovecraft was startled, but only briefly. He crouched against his writing desk, and plucked at his corduroy pants leg. "Well, I do like a man who can get to the point in a New York minute."

Secondari patted Maria's cheeks.

"We met your local head of intelligence, earlier today," said Lovecraft. "That big flying ace of yours. The State Department says that he's your master spy around here. Well, your master spy doesn't speak-a the Inglese very good. He's quite a cagey fellow. He wouldn't slip one word to us that wasn't all about giant sea-planes, and zeppelins, or civil aviation."

Secondari was silent.

"The American government is one hundred per-cent for civil aviation," said Lovecraft. "Civil aviation is a healthy development for your part of the world. Venice, Trieste, we know they'll never build a proper airport. Too old-fashioned!"

"Is your President sick?" said Secondari. "Is Wilson dying?"

"That is a scurrilous rumor," Lovecraft lied. "The British press should never have let that one slip. 'Perfidious Albion!' Now, I'm from New England, myself. A town called Providence, where we have plenty of Italians, by the way. I used to admire England, once. Boy, what a sap I was, before the War."

"Wilson ate poison in Paris. A Communist try to kill your President."

"Let's just say that mistakes were made," Lovecraft of-fered. "Now, listen to me, Colonel Secondari—is that your good ear? Forgive me. Now, let me make a few things clear to you. You see, Mr. Houdini—he's my employer—often aids the American government. But we're not that old-fash-ioned, cloak-and-dagger, European style of spy. Don't think that of us, please. We're much more like an Amateur Press Association."

"What is that?" said Secondari.

"Well, Houdini, and Bob, and me, we're American patriots, of a new, progressive kind. Through our radio, magazines, and private newspapers, we've assembled a new movement of the people who share our vision of tomorrow. We're some all-American engineers, scientists, and inventors, but mostly, well, we're writers. We aim to help our country out of a bad pinch."

Lovecraft fiddled with the sharp tip of his folded celluloid collar. "My aim, here in your country, is to gather the news and pass a few good words along—to some very high-ranking Washington officials. That is: if you can give me a few good words, sir."

Secondari warily maintained his silence. He wasn't entirely sure that he had understood such a complicated speech, uttered in American English.

Young Bob Howard returned, with a gelato clutched in his hairy fist.

"That was quick, Bob," said Lovecraft.

"I didn't want her ice cream to melt, sir."

"I just saw her little eyes flutter," said the ad-man. "Let's help her up."

Maria awoke. She spoke in a dizzy confusion of Croatian, then German, then Italian.

"Your daughter can't speak any English, I suppose?" said Lovecraft.

"No," said Secondari.

"Then we can continue speaking here in confidence," said Lovecraft. "You know what inspired me the most tonight, Colonel? It was seeing that royal personage of yours—the Duke!—taking his rightful place among his own loyal people. Now, I don't call myself a royalist conservative—sure, I used to be one, but not any more—but seeing a brand-new country like yours, placed into the firm hands of a wise, royal leader... Well, there's something about that spectacle that is really easy to write up and promote. The American public loves all that. It's charming, and so European. Mark my words, the relations between your nation and mine will improve in short order."

"That's because he's the Flying Aviator King of the Adriatic," said the cowboy.

"Exactly. That's just the hot, headline-grabbing stuff we need, Bob."

"He's a fighting King, with his sword and his fists. Maybe he could fly straight to Africa, and fight black magic!"

"Black, evil, ancient magic in Africa," Lovecraft agreed. "Centuries old. Nameless aeons of black, necrotic, mephitic magic. Say, Bob, maybe you could write up another of your fun little pieces for the *Journal of the American Magic Association*. The younger readers love those Texas tall tales."

"Well, okay, sir, maybe," said Howard doubtfully. "Mr. Houdini, he keeps me pretty busy, boxing and walking the tightrope."

"It's a paycheck," Lovecraft shrugged. "Say, Colonel, your little girl sure can tie into an ice cream."

"My Maria likes sweets," said Secondari.

"I can sure see that! Now, Colonel, we're mere strolling players here in Carnaro, we don't want to pry into your internal affairs. But there must be something that you want to tell me. Something that's juicy, and newsworthy. Something I can take straight back to our patrons in Washington."

"Yes. You can tell your master, Colonel House," said Secondari, "that we have flying radio torpedoes. Torpedoes that fly. In the dark. With radio. No one can see them."

"I've heard those rumors. Is that the truth? Those flying bombs can fly as far as Rome, eh? To the Vatican?"

"Through the Pope's door," said Secondari.

"You don't plan to cut loose with those for no good reason, do you? Mr. Houdini just met the Pope. He seemed like a nice guy, for a Catholic."

"I will tell you more news for your spies in Washington," said Secondari, straightening on the couch. "Giulio Ulivi is here with me in Fiume. The new Italian radio genius. He is as good as Marconi. Better. The inventor of the 'F-Ray.'"

"What's that?" said the cowboy. "An 'F-Ray' sounds astounding."

"A ray of death! Like the X-ray, but stronger, faster! It kills fast! Our flying torpedo, with the Ulivi F-Ray! It flies, with the radio, in the dark. Boom! Out goes the F-Ray, everyone go. Dead. Nothing left. Everyone dead."

The room was silent, except for the crisp sound of Maria Piffer crunching through the cone of her ice cream.

"That's very like H. G. Wells," judged Lovecraft. "The Wells 'land dreadnought,' that bomb that employs radioactivity. Quite a strongly opinionated political writer, Mr. Wells."

"Mr. Wells was here with us in Fiume," said Secondari. "Wells came here for the dancing girls. Wells did not believe about our Futurism. Do you believe?"

"Oh, absolutely and ineffably," said Lovecraft at once. "I heard you loud and clear."

Distant, but frenzied applause filtered into the dressing room.

"So, that's the end of our employer's performance," said Lovecraft.

"Tomorrow, they'll drop Houdini into the ocean, head first, all covered up with locks and chains," said the Texan. "So the whole world can see him drown. But he'll wiggle out of it somehow! Ha ha! Houdini always does."

Maria spoke up, in Italian. "Papa, who are these strange men? I ate my ice cream. Can we go now?"

"In just one moment, my treasure."

"Please hear us out, Colonel," said Lovecraft. "You see, we Americans believed that the Great War was the War to End All Wars. Now the League of Nations has failed, and we can see that our attempt to bring peace to the world was a rank superstition. This world only understands the virile force of arms, as wielded by a born conqueror, and..." Lovecraft smiled. "I'd better let my restless young friend tell you about that."

"He means General 'Black Jack' Pershing!" the young Texan crowed. "General Black Jack fought Pancho Villa in Texas. He fought the Great War in Europe, and Black Jack won that war, too! Because fate put us here to fight! A weakling in the battle that is life deserves to die."

"My little girl must go now," said Secondari.

"I'll be brief, Colonel. You see, General Black Jack Pershing understands—just as we do—that the next Great War is sure to come. Diplomats can't stop it, law and order can't stop it, that's useless. Now, we have some can-do, take-charge people in America—who want to reach out to Carnaro. Because we admire your integrity, your spirituality. We can see what you've achieved."

"Especially what you did about the Communists," said Bob Howard. "We aim to do that ourselves."

The Man Without Fear entered the dressing room. His face was streaming greasepaint, and a few tiny trickles of blood. He seized a plush white towel and threw it around his sweating neck.

"Did you tell him about our research project in Manhattan?" the magician said.

"Our Manhattan Project, yes, I was just getting to that," said Lovecraft.

The magician stripped out of his white tail-coat, revealing a waistcoat thick with hidden loops and pockets. He confronted Secondari. "You're the man who builds the bombs here."

"Yes."

"What if I told you," said the magician, "that in America, we have a plan to build an almighty Bomb That Will End All Bombs? A bomb so huge that it could only be tested in an American desert? Would that entertain you, Mr. Weapons Minister?"

"Yes."

"Then will you come to America with us to see that weapons-test of ours?"

Secondari, with grave deliberation, set Maria Piffer on his knee. "We are citizens of the Regency of Carnaro. We have no papers for America."

"Now, all that legal rubbish," said the magician, "is just tedious State Department paperwork, so I leave all that to my subordinates. Howard, where is the pissoir, for God's sake?"

"It's down the hall to the left," said Lovecraft.

Houdini promptly departed.

"There's no one quite like the boss," said Lovecraft reverently. "President Pershing will make Houdini the next Head of the American Secret Service. Just imagine what we'll do against World Communism, with a man like Houdini calling the shots."

"Tell me," said Secondari.

"Oh, we have visionary plans cooking in our Manhattan Project. They're half science, half fantasy, and all classified." Lovecraft adjusted his steel-rimmed spectacles. "But I can reveal this to you, sir, and I think you'll find it relevant: we use the scientific séance techniques of Dr. Cesare Lombroso as our military parapsychology."

Secondari drew and released a slow breath.

"Conventional scientists," said Lovecraft, "may scoff at our federally funded psi powers and our anti-gravity drives; and I suppose they're paid to do that, the poor things! But—well, let me speak as a professional New York public relations man."

Lovecraft turned on an electric ceiling fan, then removed his pin-striped jacket. "Let us suppose that you, sir, and a corps of your progressive, far-sighted Futurist colleagues—all clad in your charming and fantastic uniforms—were to fly to the United States? Suppose that you Futurists were to join us out on the road, in the forthcoming Pershing Presidential campaign?"

Lovecraft leaned back, examined the gilt, baroque ceiling of the Fiume City Hall, and eloquently spread his pale hands. "I can envision you Futurists flying to Chicago in a giant Italian flying pontoon boat, to be met with ticker-tape parades. Then, in a rigid airship over New York City, to be met with a symphony orchestra!" He lowered his gaze. "I know you people like that kind of pep, dash, and vim."

"Yes," said Secondari. "We like those things very much."

"In New York advertising circles, I'm known as a big-idea man. Your Regency of Carnaro is too small. That's the problem. The Land of Opportunity is a place of cosmic proportions."

"Yeah, your little utopia here is just like a pioneer town," said Bob Howard, sadly gazing at the toes of his cowboy boots. "Like some lonely place way out in the middle of nowhere, where y'all have only the dreams in your books."

"Compare that meager, mundane reality to the world you really desire," said Lovecraft. "Do you see the commonality of interests here? Imagine what we might achieve!"

D'ANNUNZIO IN FIUME WITH ARMED FORCES

Brings Machine Guns and Armored Cars in Defiance of Italian Government Orders.

ROME, Sept. 12.—Gabriele d'Annunzio, the Italian poet-aviator, arrived in Fiume from Ronchi this afternoon with detachments of grenadiers and arditi provided with machine guns and armored automobiles, according to reports reaching this city tonight. The movement was made in violation of orders from the Government. No disorders were reported up till late tonight.

Government officials have been instructed to investigate recent demonstrations at Fiume and determine who was responsible for them.

VENICE, Sept. 12.—Gabriele d'Annunzio on Thursday night secretly joined the body of Italian Volunteers which entered and occupied Fiume today.

It is reported that General " Peppino " Garibaldi is among the volunteers.

Captain Gabriele d'Annunzio, who distinguished himself as an Italian aviator during the war, has been one of the most ardent advocates of Italian claims to territory on the eastern shore of the Adriatic. In the course of the controversy over the disposition of Fiume at the Peace Conference in May, and later after the resignation of Premier Orlando, appeals were made to the Italian people by Captain d'Annunzio, who urged that Italy fight for her " just claims." Reports reaching London on Thursday said that serious fighting between Italian and Jugoslav soldiers had taken place at Fiume, and that allied units had been compelled to intervene.

TO THE FIUME STATION
★
CHRISTOPHER BROWN

"Imagine a
city that experiments
with the grain of the material."
—Bruno Argento, 2008

ON SUNDAY, SEPTEMBER 14, 1919, the *New York
Times* reported the state of the world as viewed
from Manhattan on that weekend ten months after
the end of the Great War. One-hundred and thirty-
thousand war refugees ordered to leave Austria. Unrest
in Boston as Governor Coolidge fought the police strike
by sending out volunteer militia and state guards to put
down rowdy crowds with truck-mounted machine guns.
President Wilson visited Seattle, confronting a huge gathering
of angry Wobblies with "giant" Secret Service agents and "a
little army of sturdy Boy Scouts" who beat back the "great throng
suddenly realizing its power" as they demanded Wilson "release
all political prisoners"—including Socialist presidential candidate
Eugene Debs, who Wilson's government had imprisoned for
speaking out against the war. An armed mob in Pueblo, Colorado,
seized two Mexican farm hands from the local jail and hung them

from a bridge at the edge of town. In a major speech, British Prime Minister David Lloyd George issued a call to "build up the new world" for which the fallen of the war had died—a future in which "labor shall have its just reward and indolence alone shall suffer want"—echoing Wilson's call in Tacoma the day before for "all the great free peoples of the world to underwrite civilization." And in technology news, an airplane managed to carry nine passengers from Syracuse in less than three hours—and even cook a meal on board! Buried on page 12, between anachronistic stories about the price of foxskins in St. Louis and the purple silk-lined yellow coyote skin gifted to the Prince of Wales on his visit to Edmonton, was this item of foreign news:

D'ANNUNZIO IN FIUME
WITH ARMED FORCES
Brings Machine Guns and Armored Cars in Defiance of
Italian Government Orders.

ROME, Sept. 12—Gabriele D'Annunzio, the Italian poet-aviator, arrived in Fiume from Ronchi this afternoon with detachments of grenadiers and Arditi provided with machine guns and armored automobiles, according to reports reaching this city tonight. The movement was made in violation of orders from the government. No disorders were reported till late tonight.

That is not to suggest that *Pirate Utopia* is a true story. It's an alternate history of a momentarily successful attempt to conjure an alternate future, written by the author's Italian multiverse doppelgänger. Given the wide variations among consensus reality's histories of Fiume, Sterling's speculative counterfactual proves a useful tool to divine deeper truths about this extravagant deviation from post-Westphalian convention that, when viewed from a century's distance, proves to be an important lodestar of our own immanent tomorrows—and how we can go about rewriting them.

The real world's Gabriele D'Annunzio—the Prophet of *Pirate Utopia*—was a global celebrity of the *Proud Tower* era before WWI, a decadent poet, playwright, and novelist whose works were popular on both sides of the Atlantic, and an adherent of Nietzsche who transformed himself into a bona fide world historical Übermensch at the dawn of the twentieth century. A longtime flying buff who had flown with Wilbur Wright in 1908, when the war broke out he incredibly became a military aviator in his fifties, losing an eye in aerial combat, and then using the constraints of his partially blinded convalescence to innovate a new mode of literary composition. When the political brokers at Versailles gave the former Austro-Hungarian port of Fiume to the new nation of Yugoslavia they had just patched together on the conference room table, the burgeoning Italian nationalist movements saw a failure of politics—Fiume to them was a historical part of Italy, an old territory of Venice still dominated by an Italian population that expected repatriation. After an auspicious reading of the cards by an American-born princess, D'Annunzio grabbed the opportunity to accept the Italian-Fiumans' invitation and round up a crew of demobilized troops to correct this error of the state through bold action, anticipating that by restoring this piece of Italian glory, he would inspire a movement that would do the same with the whole country. He was partially right.

D'Annunzio, aided by "Ace of Hearts" Guido Keller, a fellow Ardito aviator who kept a pet eagle and liked to take naked walks on the beach, managed to take Fiume with just 186 veterans and a few barely serviceable surplus vehicles—pushing through the nominal opposition with bluster, patriotic appeals, and a few rounds of gunfire. But he was unable to work out mutually agreeable terms for the adoption of Fiume by the mother country. In the absence of clear politico-legal status, Fiume became a temporary autonomous zone to which war-forged modernists flocked from all over the world—Futurists and proto-fascists, Dadaists and syndicalists, free lovers and strident Bolsheviks, radio innovators and desperadoes, all drawn by D'Annunzio's calls from his hotel balcony and the press releases put out by his team of international poets turned public relations hacks. At night, Dionysus reigned in the libertine *festa* that

would never end, and in the daytime, the new Fiumans rewrote the social contract with a fresh constitution that would make the means of production communally managed, obliterate conventional divisions of labor, and elevate aesthetics to the point of making music a central principle of the state.

Real-world Fiume's candle burned out after fifteen months, but the Fiume of *Utopia Pirata* isn't bound by such constraints. Sterling imagines a different outcome—one where the mix of technological innovation, futurist ideas and liberated territory creates a moment in which forward-thinking people can seize the controls and steer the world towards their vision of a better future—or at least one juiced with more imaginative vitality. Sterling's alt.Fiume is uninfected by the naive idealizations of contemporary anarchist depictions of D'Annunzio's experiment, showing the dark fascist specters lurking behind the Waldropian fun-house mirror—and the deluded hubris intrinsic to all applied utopias. At the same time, the story's whimsy lubricates the narrative tumblers that unlock the gates of "what if?" wonder and invite us to invent our own ending—for the story and for our own selves. "Compare that meager, mundane reality to the world you really desire," says H. P. Lovecraft the ad-man. After the chuckles stop, the provocation remains.

The text of *Pirate Utopia* looks backward, but the story is more cyberpunk than steampunk—a work that shares DNA with Sterling's seminal 1980s novel *Islands in the Net*, with its global archipelago of future Fiumes, and applies Sterling's more recent observations about the ways network culture liberates the timeline of our minds from the constraints of historiographically sanctioned official narratives. *Pirate Utopia* travels back to Fiume to open a portal that looks forward from our own destabilized present, a liminal now whose 2019 just came into range looking a lot like the pre-apocalyptic truncheon show of that 1919 *New York Times*. But where D'Annunzio and his interwar peers were inspired by the romantic visions of generations of continental philosophers, we are stuck with a world governed by the more dismal (and now discredited) science of neoclassical economics. And with science fiction, and all its pulp-tethered limitations.

The Zeitgeist surfers of Fiume rode the long waves of speculative social science that charged European political change from the Enlightenment through the Cold War. Rousseau's revelation that human nature could be improved by redesigning the structure of society uncorked a few centuries of whiteboard utopias that managed to get beta-tested in real life, from Saint-Simon's prescient visions of techno-meritocracy to Fourier's communal phalanxes of work based on joy and Marx's elusive communist paradise. These utopian postulates provided the aspirational dipole to Darwinian pragmatism and pushed Western societies in the long-term pursuit of an idealized tomorrow. But the mechanized violence of the twentieth century, the corrupt failure of the Soviet experiment, and the quotidian demands of capital extinguished the aurora of those ideas, leaving us a "politics practiced as a branch of advertising" whose pretenses of diversity mask a resigned nihilism and the exhaustion of hope. And so the business of inventing better worlds falls to sf writers, most of whom find it is dystopia that pays the bills.

The author of *Pirate Utopia* is someone who walks the talk, busy the past decade bushwhacking an alternate future in the fabric of his own life—busting out of generic confinement to practice speculative design as a freshly potent narrative mode, living the laptop-based existence of an itinerant cybernomad in the ethereal realm he helped create, and even occupying an Italian mirror world version of himself, the Turinese *scrittore di fantascienza* Bruno Argento, who was the actual author of the story you just read. If you catch one of Bruce/Bruno's many public speaking appearances, you may hear him talk of his aspiration "to write a regional novel of Planet Earth." In *Pirate Utopia* and other recent European counterfactuals like "Black Swan" and "The Parthenopean Scalpel," it's evident that he is already doing that, in installments—in this episode, glimpsing a different American future through atemporal Italian portals. While no bona fide utopian prescriptions have yet emerged from Sterling's trenchant speculative diagnostics, one wonders what he would do if we gave him a liberated city-state to run.

INTERVIEW WITH
BRUCE STERLING
★
RICK KLAW

*While in
Austin for the annual
SXSW Interactive conference,
Bruce Sterling sat down with editor
Rick Klaw. The pair discussed many
things including alternate history and ego,
Rijeka, Gabriele D'Annunzio, fantascienza,
fascism, H. P. Lovecraft, torpedoes, and, of course,
Pirate Utopia.*

Rick Klaw: People who have read your work before might be a bit surprised by *Pirate Utopia* because it's not the hard science fiction of your novels. It has much more of the cultural aspects present in your short fiction.

Bruce Sterling: This is Dieselpunk. It's an alternate history story. It's like *Difference Engine* or other alternate history stories. I wrote an alternate history story more recently that was in *Twelve Tomorrows*. Every year [the *MIT Technology Review*] do their science fiction issue and I've been the editor twice. This year I wrote an alternate history story about a guy with an Antikythera device, which is this lost Greek calculating device. I've actually written a lot of alternative history stuff. It's usually very much about technology.

Pirate Utopia has got a killer F-Ray and a flying aerial torpedo in it. Not to mention cheap, mass-produced single-shot handguns. The lead character's an engineer, it's engineering fiction, military engineering fiction. It's got a lot of dress-up stuff; I mean, guys are wearing trenchcoats, with a lot of careful descriptions of Italian Futurist-styled uniforms and all kinds of cool period gear: megaphones, wireless sets, biplanes. I think if you're a dieselpunk fan or a steampunk fan you would find that rather simpatico. If you're interested in that period, it's a refreshing setting.

Klaw: What interests you so much about this particular alternate history?

Sterling: I've actually been through the area a lot that's described in this story, and Rijeka, the former Fiume, is an area I pass through very often on my way from the Balkans to Italy. I've come to know that city very well. It really is a haunted place. It's just a peculiar Adriatic port. What went on there during the period that I'm describing was really one of the strangest episodes of political extremism in European history. Really a weird thing, and surprisingly little-known. So I was hanging out in Rijeka, and I thought, "I'm gonna write something about what happened here." I knew people there and they were interviewing me. "So, American Science Fiction Writer, what's your next project?" and I said, "I'm gonna write some science fiction set here in Rijeka." People were just thunderstruck, like "Why would he do it?" but also impressed. There's surprisingly a lot of Croatian science fiction fandom. Rijeka has a society which was literally split between Yugoslavia and Italy in a very violent way. I've spent a lot of time in both Yugoslavia and Italy, so it's an area that culturally interests me a lot.

Klaw: How much do the events in the book match up to the true history of Fiume?

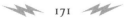

Sterling: They're very close until they begin to deviate as my hero's machinations have more and more of an effect on history. Because he's never aware that he's a major figure—in fact he has no idea that he's managed to sidetrack Mussolini and Hitler. That's just collateral damage. He's just trying to build some bombs here. Torpedoes are what really interests the guy. In our own line of history he's a dead man, obviously, but in the story's line of alternate history, he's a Turinese engineer with a gift, and a chip on his shoulder. So he is able to emphasize the technological aspects of the Fiume Revolution more than just hanging around, reciting poetry, and taking drugs, which is what they mostly did. In our original timeline there was a torpedo factory in Fiume, but the Allies managed to shut it down. The poetic rebels just didn't have anybody with the technical chops to hack a factory and get it going.

Klaw: You're talking about in our real history, there was a torpedo factory there?

Sterling: Yeah.

Klaw: But that would have been in the '20s.

Sterling: It was an Austro-Hungarian torpedo factory. There are still remnants of it there. They were major torpedo makers…I mean, they made a lot of armaments for the Austro-Hungarian Navy.

Klaw: And you've visited that factory?

Sterling: Yeah, we were there, Jasmina [Tešanović] and I were both there for a big cyberpunk event, which was held on Tito's rusty old yacht in the Fiume Harbor. I was lecturing the people of Fiume on their own history, which they know very little about. They're like most people. It's like telling people in Austin about Colonel [Edward M.] House, who basically ran the U.S.

Government while Woodrow Wilson was demented by a stroke. House lived in Austin. And nobody here would know that. He's not a household figure.

Klaw: Have others written about the pirates of Fiume?

Sterling: Peter Lamborn Wilson wrote a famous work on pirate utopias. And there were a number of other pirate utopias, but Fiume is one of the most famous and actually had real pirates; they were stealing the living daylights out of stuff.

Klaw: Pirates think everything works like that.

Sterling: The Strike of the Hand Committee was very much a smash-and-grab-style organization. They stole tons of stuff: entire ships, herds of horses, diesel fuel, weaponry, all kinds of things.

Klaw: Alternate histories about this region and World War I are practically an Italian subgenre.

Sterling: Yeah. A lot exist. There's a work of Italian science fiction called *The Biplanes of D'Annunzio* [by Luca Masali], which was written about ten years ago. It starred Gabriele D'Annunzio, who is also a character in my book.

Klaw: What's up with all the nicknames in *Pirate Utopia*?

Sterling: For some mythic reason I decided to refer to everybody by their epithets, so the hero Lorenzo Secondari is called Pirate Engineer by most people, and D'Annunzio is called The Prophet, and the Ace of Hearts is actually a guy named Guido Keller in real life, and the Jewish Economist *was* a Jewish economist, and The Constitutionalist, they're all real, and the Art Witch, of course, is Luisa Casati.

Klaw: It's all very pulp in a superhero kind of way.

Sterling: Within Fiume people referred to D'Annunzio as Il Vate, which is sort of the Prophetic Poet. D'Annunzio liked to rename people, and there was this atmosphere of unreality that came from living in the D'Annunzio orbit. Everything was sort of super-eloquent and kind of renamed. So if you were one of the pirates, the Fiume pirates, you were known as *Uskoki*. Nobody had any idea what the hell that was. The Uskoki were fifteenth-century Christian Adriatic pirates who had fought the Moslems of the Ottoman Empire. D'Annunzio, a super well-read guy, knew this, so he's rounding up all his men and coming up with these bizarre rituals, many of which have, of course, been forgotten, but some of which became super-influential. The Roman fascist salute was invented in Fiume by D'Annunzio. "We're not gonna salute the way we did during the war, we're going to salute in the old-fashioned Roman way," and they're like, "Okay, Vate! Anything else?" "Yeah! Instead of saying 'Hip-hip-hooray,' we're going to say 'Eia, eia, alalà,'" and the fascists ended up shouting this all the time. Certain fascist theme songs were invented in Fiume, like "Giovinezza," which is the famous fascist marching song. A lot of the leaders of the fascist group, including Mussolini, matriculated in Fiume. They would hang out there, do drugs, have sex, and soak up some fascist ideology. Marconi got a divorce in Fiume. It was a funny place. It was like Batista Cuba in some ways: everything was legal; everything was permitted.

Klaw: When I last interviewed you in the early 2000s, we were talking at the time about the influence of Texas on your writing. You've lived in Europe now for ten years or so; has it had a similar effect on your writing?

Sterling: Yeah, I have alter-ego writers now, who I rely on. I mean there's Bruno Argento, who's the Turinese Bruce Sterling, so my new Italian collection, which is called *Utopia Pirata,* has *I Racconti di Bruno Argento* as a subtitle. I actually see writing these Italian stories as my attempt to add something to the Italian tradition of *fantascienza*. I know there's been quite a lot of fantastic writing in

Turin over the years. Calvino was from Turin and Primo Levi was from Turin. Right now, although there's a lot of science fiction fandom in Turin, there are no such prominent Turinese fantasy writers, except for me, or rather my alter-ego, Bruno Argento. I also have a Serbian alter-ego writer of fantastyka, who's called Boris Srebro.

Klaw: Are these very public alter-egos?

Sterling: Yeah. I've been talking to people about it, but mostly it's just something I put on the top of the page as I write. "I'm going to write with the Boris Srebro voice in this story." So my story "Kiosk," which is set in a future Belgrade, is a Boris Srebro story. But this particular story, *Pirate Utopia*, is actually kind of a Boris Srebro/Bruno Argento mash-up, because it's about Yugoslavia and Italy at the same time.

Klaw: Are you writing in other languages, or still just in English?

Sterling: I write entirely in English because I don't have the chops to write a proper, literary Italian, and Serbian will always be out of my reach. I'm getting a little better at it. I can read Italian and I've got a sincere interest in fantascienza. I know what fantascienza's about, what the themes are, the kind of historical roots of it, and why Italian popular genre writing is as it was. So I wouldn't call myself a scholar of popular Italian literature, but I know at least enough about it that I can get away with creating it. I think I have a friendly reception from the Italian SF community for writing stuff about their interests. Which can be a little weird, as I try to imagine an Italian science fiction writer coming to Texas and deciding that he wants to write westerns and live in Austin. But maybe that would work—maybe he'd do great westerns, like great spaghetti westerns. Or maybe he'd just put a foot wrong and make a fool of himself. Or, it might be well-received work back where he came from, but it would be rather difficult for someone in Austin to say, "This Italian guy is telling us stuff about Austin that we ourselves didn't know." But I think it's doable. I can get away with it because I write about a fantastic Italy rather than a real Italy. If I tried to write a modern novel about everyday life in Italy I think my foreignness would be more obvious. I can actually do these alternate Italys or future Italys and they have a freshness to them. Italian readers are just kind of like, "Where the heck did that come from?"

Klaw: And the foreignness actually could heighten the science fiction.

Sterling: Yeah; it heightens the exoticism of it. I feel like there's some room for work there because one of the most popular comic book characters in Italian comics publishing, *fumetti* publishing, is a heroic cowboy named Tex. Tex Willer. Tex has been around for over sixty years.

Klaw: I've got a Tex collection sitting on my tablet.

Sterling: If you're in Italy, Tex looms very large; he's all over the place, so yeah, this is Italy appropriating stuff from Texas. Even though Tex Willer actually lives in Arizona, it's not much of an Arizona: spaceships, giant rattlesnakes, Aztec mummies, all the cool fumetti fantasy elements you could possibly want. Fumetti are very powerful within the Italian fantasy tradition. I mean, fantascienza is not exactly equivalent to SF. It doesn't convey the exact same social function that science fiction does within American society. Fantascienza really is a kind of science fantasy, and it appeals to elements of Italian popular culture that cut through reality at a somewhat different angle. There's a closeness between crime writing, historical fiction writing, and science fiction writing in Italy that you wouldn't see in the U.S. People in those genres don't really hang out with each other a whole lot in the U.S., but within Italian science fiction culture, they're quite close. They share the same publishers and it's a proper thing to be Valerio Evangelisti, for instance, and write both historical thrillers and science fiction.

Klaw: Is it much more like it is in England? I know in England writers can jump genres easier than in the United States.

Sterling: A lot of it has to do with the small scale of the language. The markets are not big enough to afford big iron-clad genres. So if you're a popular writer, and you're not a literary writer in Italy, then you're in a class of popular writing, and it doesn't really matter if you write a murder mystery that has science fiction elements or whatever. It's just looser. I mean, this bothers people in Italy that are very scholarly, that know a lot about science fiction. In some ways they are scratching their heads over it. "Why are we doing it this way?" But I think that's a sign of their creative vitality. Others would imagine that Italian science fiction people were super-literary because Calvino's famous and he was a Nobel Prize-caliber writer. But actual Italian fantasy subculture people are way into SF for its gaudy pop culture aspects. They really like B-movies, horror, scandal stuff, they like the spaghetti western aspects of it because they're fed up with their high-flown literary writing. They want some stuff with some guts. It's why Joe Lansdale is a super-popular guy there. Italians don't want to read a lot of Stanislaw Lem—it doesn't have enough vitamins in it.

Klaw: It sounds similar to the U.S. fascination with *Star Wars*. Many of the fans come to it for "its gaudy pop culture aspects."

Sterling: There's not vast swarms of Italian fans, and there's more of a regional variety in Italian society than you would think. Roman fans and Milanese fans are somewhat poles apart—I mean, there are really Roman writers and Milanese writers, and I'm willing to go with that. I've been struggling recently to write an Italian story which is for the Roman group, the Connectivist writers. The Roman Connettivismo is much more into cyberpunk than the Milanese guys, so as a Turinese writer, I'm now trying to branch out and do some work which is more Roman, and that's surprisingly hard for me.

Klaw: Do you have any plans to write another novel-length alternate history in the vein of *Difference Engine*?

Sterling: My editor for *Utopia Pirata*, Giuseppe Lippi, has been encouraging me to write a novel. He thought that *Utopia Pirata* would make a perfectly acceptable novel, but it ends in a peculiar way, because the hero's going off to join the Manhattan Project with H. P. Lovecraft. So you think, "Well, wait a minute!" Obviously the big trouble's just now starting, and Lovecraft is promising him, "Join us and we'll do fantastic stuff!" But I decided to cut it off with that moment, because it makes a statement about the nature, the appeal, of fascism. How lofty and spiritual it is, and how people come to agree with it, like they get hypnotized by the inhumanity of it, and the scope of it. Fascism does have the appeal of science fiction in some ways. As Norman Spinrad pointed out when he wrote his *Iron Dream* many years ago, which was about Hitler as a small-scale sci-fi writer, there's this brotherly feeling between certain kinds of political ecstatic cult politics and the "sense of wonder" of reality-bending in science fiction. They both supply a lot of crypto-religious loftiness of "What if it's really like that?" and "What if we could really…" and then it jumps to "Italians, you have your empire!"

This awesomeness covers a lot of political shabbiness. When you study how fascism was actually carried out as a practice, there was this massive, ecstatic life with the huge rallies and the flowers and the sacrifice and the noble fall and the martial ardor and all that, but at the same time fascism was really a grimy little favor-driven society. It was not a prosperous society. You really had to depend on the party boss to get you all kinds of favors, and to get your children educated, to buy a house. You had to ingratiate yourself with this one-party state. There was this tremendous loftiness on one scale and on another there was this pathetic, grimy quality that robbed people of dignity. These two aspects feed off of one another in a remarkable way. It took me a long time to figure it out. I was very polite about fascism because being a Texan trying to quiz Italians about fascism was exactly like being an Italian and going up to Lansdale's hometown and asking about the KKK: "So, white hoods, eh? What were those made of? What did they burn the crosses with?"

Rick: (laughing) "Why do you think I should know?"

Sterling: Yeah. Especially in Turin, which is very much a city of the left and was bitterly opposed to Mussolini for most of his reign. The Turinese really suffered a lot under the fascist regime. The wounds have faded away; the new generation knows very little about it, but it was degrading and painful for a lot of people, so I didn't want to tread on their feet. On the other hand, fascism really was one of the most successful social innovations that Italy has ever had. You think of Italy as the birthplace of the Renaissance, but fascism spread over all of Europe very quickly and had followers in every society, including Britain and the U.S. It was a super-influential political philosophy, and the embers are not that far below the surface because people don't understand its allure.

Klaw: The book ended there because sometimes when you push something, like the whole thing with Lovecraft, it's in danger of becoming so absurd that you lose sight of what you were trying to do in the first place.

Sterling: Yeah, it's difficult to handle that. Lovecraft actually interests me a lot because he's such a lively figure now. He's in both Modern Library and Library of America. People are writing all kinds of Lovecraft pastiches, and even guys in the American Right Wing like to talk about Lovecraft. Cthulhu runs for president every year and it's always funny. Lovecraft's really coming into his own as a literary figure. I can easily imagine writing a Lovecraft fascist parody that would be horrifying in kind of a Thomas Ligotti vein, where Lovecraft really is a fascist, and he's taking over Providence and kicking all of the Italians out, or whatever Lovecraft would have done if anyone had ever given him political power.

Klaw: Well, you wrote a Cthulhu story.

Sterling: It was about nuclear disarmament talks where all of the nuclear disarmament stuff is actually Cthulhu mythos horrors. It was called "The Unthinkable."

Klaw: I seem to remember you being very proud of the fact that you got to be in the Lovecraft Circle.

Sterling: I took Lovecraft quite seriously and still do. I actually know a lot about Lovecraft and his methods. I've read all his letters. He's influential in a lot of ways. People make fun of him, but for the wrong reasons. They don't understand why someone like Michel Houellebecq would write about Lovecraft and take Lovecraft very seriously. Houellebecq is probably the most prominent French novelist working right now and a big Lovecraft devotee. He's written scholarly works about Lovecraft from a very metaphysical point of view. It's all on Cosmic Horror, and the emptiness of this, that, and the other. So I think I could have continued the *Pirate Utopia* story, but I would have had to write it in a Lovecraftian vein. I don't really like writing cosmic horror all that much, and I really wouldn't have wanted to spend that much time under Lovecraft's skin, as it were. Lovecraft actually did work for Houdini, and Houdini did work for the U.S. Secret Service, so it's not that far-fetched to imagine Lovecraft involved with the espionage community. Ghost writer. Propagandist. Dirty tricks artist. I could easily imagine Lovecraft as a psychological operations guy, a Psy-Ops guy, because he's very erudite and surprisingly charming. People talk about him as if he were an emotional basket case, but they've never read his letters and realized how many people were relying on him for pep talk. For most people in Lovecraft's circle, he was Uncle Theobald, a figure of strength. He was very much an inspirational and an avuncular figure, someone to trust. He couldn't earn a living, but nobody could—times were quite tough.

Klaw: Why use Lovecraft as opposed to a European figure of the time?

Sterling: I think it's me tipping my own American hat there. The political message there is that "it can happen here," in the words of Sinclair Lewis who wrote a famous warning about fascism in American society. It wouldn't be called fascism if it were to happen here; I think Lewis is right to say that it would arrive wrapped in the flag and carrying the cross under American circumstances. Fascism is an attempt to make politics metaphysical and poetic that actually ends up creating a lot of crippling difficulties for people in their everyday lives. You can't aspire to this level of cosmic glee, I guess you would call it, and actually do normal stuff like bake bread, deliver the mail, clean out the plumbing, be nice to your mom, volunteer down at the old folks' home. None of that mundane life compares to, like, Conquering Libya, so everything is weirdly distorted.

I think the Italians are somewhat given to that, they did more or less invent it. It does have a lot of roots within their own society and their own society is super-influential in some ways. They're a very culturally inventive people. So it was a pleasure to write this because I really felt in some ways I was getting something off my chest. Just like: Why is Rijeka like Rijeka? This little town with so much trouble packed into it. In some ways they were wise because they were also the first anti-fascist city. The people of Rijeka were the first to just get fed up. Knock it off! We just can't handle it any more. They chased the fascists out of their town, basically. They never did the same thing again in Rijeka. Even when their town was taken over by fascists in the war, they weren't particularly en-thusiastic about it. They were like the first carriers of a disease, and after that sorrow they were like, "Oh, lord. I don't want to hear about it." Even today there's something jaded about them. It's as if they got it out of their system in a major way. I could easily live in Rijeka. There's just something cool about the Adriatic. It's like Galveston in a lot of ways: run-down cool old buildings, palm trees, lots of oranges, lots of fresh fish.

Klaw: No hurricanes, though.

Sterling: They've got some heavy weather. They don't have

hurricanes, but they have mistrals. They have earthquakes. A lot of earthquakes in the Adriatic. It's a turbulent part of the world, but Rijeka's pretty peaceful now. It's not a big town. They had a lot of stuff piled up on top of them that they just couldn't...nobody could have dealt with that burden. They went through the whole gamut of it. Strange business for them. One wishes them well. I do spend a lot of time there. We're fond of them. I feel like I owe them a debt in some way. I don't blame them for what happened to them; on the contrary, I kind of admire them for their ability to get through life without having to make huge claims for themselves.

Klaw: Was *Pirate Utopia* your way to bring attention to the region's history?

Sterling: I don't know. Is *Difference Engine* a way to call attention to the difference engine? Yeah, and in fact that book did call a lot of attention to the difference engine, Lady Ada and her computers. The Babbage legend is now part and parcel of our common discourse. The Babbage computer project was a lot smaller and more obscure than the really very serious and sinister political developments that went on in Rijeka. It's a political warning for an era of daffy political excess, which is what we've got. Our politics have lost touch with conventional reality.

RECONSTRUCTING THE FUTURE: NOTES ON DESIGN

★

JOHN COULTHART

"We will find
abstract equivalents for
all the forms and elements of
the universe, and then we will com-
bine them according to the caprice of our
inspiration."

THE QUOTE IS from the Futurist manifesto written in 1915 by artists Fortunato Depero and Giacomo Balla, a document the pair titled with hyperbole typical of their avant-garde colleagues, *The Futurist Reconstruction of the Universe*. When you look into the history of the Futurists one of the first things you notice is a singular lack of modesty or restraint, so the idea of planning an artistic reconstruction of the universe was a natural extrapolation of the most energetic of all the art movements that enlivened the 1920s.

Energy—especially of the machine variety—sets the Futurists apart from some of the more inward-looking and formulaic Modernists working before and after the First World War. There's no Expressionist angst to be found in the artists and

writers who celebrated the "cleansing" value of modern warfare, but all the avant-gardists of the period share with the Modernist writers the sense that everything which had seemed fixed in the Nineteenth Century was now to be examined afresh: questioned, broken apart, then either discarded or pieced together in startling new forms. *Pirate Utopia* isn't the first book I've worked on which has mined this fervid decade for artistic potential, but the graphic novel I spent most of the 1990s creating with David Britton, *Lord Horror: Reverbstorm*, pastiches the styles of the Cubist and Expressionist painters, especially Picasso, along with borrowings from the Bauhaus designers. *Pirate Utopia* forced me to look much more closely at the Futurists than I had done before.

The Futurists may have desired a reconstruction of the universe but Futurist painting still involved the very old and very traditional application of oil paint on canvas. Luigi Russolo, Umberto Boccioni, Tullio Crali, and others are all exceptional artists but their paintings—blurred and nebulous as many of them are in their depiction of speed and movement—can't easily be co-opted by a designer looking for black-and-white images. Fortunato Depero, on the other hand, was a designer and illustrator as well as a painter, and it's his bold, often cartoon-like graphics which I've adapted for many of the illustrations in this book. While most of Depero's contemporaries remained wedded to their canvases, Depero attempted to live up to his manifesto by bringing his own brand of Futurism to textile design, furniture, stage sets, tapestries, children's toys, even sketches for Marinetti's *Manifesto of Futurist Cooking*. (To make "Chicken Fiat," fill a chicken with ball bearings, roast it, then serve with whipped cream.)

Depero's later work, some of which involved advertising design in Italy and magazine illustration in New York, featured hand-drawn Futurist alphabets, a set of which provide the headings in *Pirate Utopia*. Depero's print work extended to radical page layouts (the Futurists eagerly trampled on several centuries of Italian typesetting tradition) which he presented in *Depero Futurista* (1927), a book whose heavy card covers were bound together with a pair of brashly utilitarian nuts and bolts. The page design of

Pirate Utopia alludes to some of Depero's layouts although there's nothing here that's quite as wild as the Futurists were when they exploded the conventions of book design. Depero's art is probably best known to modern Italians via his many Campari ads, and his design of the Campari Soda bottle which is still in use today. The Soviet avant-garde would have scorned the use of art in the service of capitalism but Depero declared, somewhat presciently, that "the art of the future will be largely advertising." And to extend an imaginary debate, he might also have noted that Soviet art was in any case merely advertising for the Revolution. To his credit, Depero's advertising work retains his angled and spiky Futurist stylings, and some of the Campari ads and magazine designs have also been adapted for illustrations in this book.

Elsewhere in the book there's a nod to Soviet Constructivism on the cover, with colours, letterforms, aircraft formation, and a flag-waving crowd that suggest the propaganda posters of the period. If this seems at odds with the Futurism within, consider it a hijacking (or pirating) of the graphics of a rival ideology (in addition to being a request from the editors...), just as Secondari pirates (or hijacks) the Lancia-Ansaldo IZM from the unfortunate Communists. That armoured car is accurately depicted, incidentally, as are the Caproni bombers on the cover and inside the book. The title spread is adapted from a cover design by "Golia" (Eugenio Colmo) for a children's book, *Ipergenio il disinventore* (1925) by Giovanni Bertinetti. Golia and Bertinetti lived in Turin, where their book was also published, so in addition to being a splendid piece of industrial illustration there's a connection with Secondari's home town.

One of the pleasures of working on *Pirate Utopia* was discovering more about the historical as well as the aesthetic background. I was familiar with the exploits of Gabriele D'Annunzio (The Prophet) via Philippe Jullian's biography, less so with other characters such as Guido Keller (The Ace of Hearts) who was as spirited in our timeline as he is in the fictional one. And I was delighted when I realised that the Art Witch was the remarkable Marchesa Casati, a woman whose vast fortune was disbursed in part by commissioning portraits from every artist she met, Depero among them. I hope her kohl-eyed ghost appreciates my attempt. Many of the smaller graphics—the Hungarian radio logo, the Fiume postage stamp—are authentic items, as is the flag of the short-lived Republic of Carnaro whose motto translates as "Who is against us?"

If you reread this book—and I hope that you do—you don't have to make a meal of it unless you wish to fully experience the Futurist ethos. (Adventurous carnivores might try Marinetti's "Excited Pig": skin a whole salami, cook it in strong espresso coffee, then flavour with eau de cologne.) But you could always make yourself a Campari cocktail—there's a choice of Negroni, Garibaldi or Americano—or, if you can find one, pour yourself a Campari Soda. Fortunato Depero would approve, I'm sure.

BIOGRAPHIE/

WARREN ELLIS is the internationally bestselling author of the graphic novels *Transmetropolitan*, *Fell*, *Red*, and *Planetary*, and the novels *Gun Machine* and *Crooked Little Vein*. His graphic novel *Iron Man: Extremis* was the basis for the blockbuster *Iron Man 3* movie. He has written for *Vice* and *Wired UK* and is currently at work on various projects. Ellis lives near London in Southend-On-Sea.

JOHN COULTHART is the World Fantasy Award-winning illustrator and designer of the iconic *Steampunk* anthology series, the *Thackery T. Lambshead Pocket Guide to Eccentric & Discredited Diseases*, *Lovecraft's Monsters*, *Lord Horror: Reverbstorm*, and *The Haunter of the Dark and Other Grotesque Visions*. He was the Artist Guest of Honor at Ars Necronomica in 2015. Coulthart lives in Manchester, England.

World Fantasy Award nominee CHRISTOPHER BROWN's debut novel *Tropic of Kansas*, about Americans trying to create their own liberated city-states, is forthcoming from HarperVoyager in 2017. His other fiction and criticism can be found at CHRISTOPHER-BROWN.COM.

Mojo Press co-founder RICK KLAW is an editor, pop culture historian, reviewer, social media maven, and optimistic curmudgeon. His most recent editorial projects include *The Apes of Wrath*, *Rayguns Over Texas*, *Hap and Leonard*, and *Hap and Leonard Ride Again*. Klaw lives in Austin, Texas.